Blame it on the heat...?

Jake's mouth came down on hers and he continued to kiss her. Elizabeth grew dizzy again, though this time from sheer desire, and not the stifling Texas temperature. Still, it was probably a hundred degrees inside the car.

She didn't know why Jake had this effect on her, but she was a mass of quivering sexual awareness whenever he looked at her. And touched her. And kissed her in a way that said, *I'm taking you to bed....*

When his hand tangled with her dress hem and connected with a bare thigh, Elizabeth knew she was in trouble. His lips dropped to her neck, while his fingers skimmed higher to graze the silk underwear she'd foolishly worn on a hot day. His thumb dipped beneath the elastic and touched—

Elizabeth struggled to sit up in the car. "Jake, we can't do this here...."

Jake grinned and pulled her close. "How 'bout we go back to my house," he suggested lazily. "I could show you my quilts." The expression in his eyes was clear.

Pure unadulterated lust.

Which meant only one thing to Elizabeth—time to get out of T

Dear Reader,

Welcome to Beauville, Texas! *Blame It on Cowboys* is the first book in my BOOTS & BEAUTIES miniseries, which takes place in a small Texas town. I didn't plan to write so many books about Beauville. One day I was in the middle of Jake and Elizabeth's story and—presto—a cast of characters appeared, many of whom deserved a romance of their own.

I hope you'll look for more of my *Blame It on...* novels in 2001. A pregnant waitress and a handful of wild cowboys arrive in February, in #819 *Blame It on Babies*, which begins with a wedding you'll want to attend.

Then my first Harlequin single title, *Blame It on Texas*, will be released in March. You'll see what happened to Elizabeth and Jake, plus learn a few of the town's best-kept secrets, when the Good Night Drive In is turned into a retirement home and Dustin Jones, former cowhand at the Dead Horse Ranch, meets up with his first love.

Pookie, the incontinent Shih Tzu in *Blame It on Cowboys*, is no fictional character. I saw his picture on the Internet and adopted him three years ago from a rescue organization. I'm sure he'd like to hear from readers, too!

Sincerely,

Kristine Rolofson

P.O. Box 323
Peace Dale, RI 02883

Books by Kristine Rolofson

HARLEQUIN TEMPTATION
692—THE WRONG MAN IN WYOMING
712—THE RIGHT MAN IN MONTANA
765—BILLY AND THE KID

Kristine Rolofson
BLAME IT ON COWBOYS

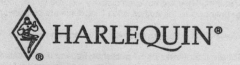

HARLEQUIN®

TORONTO • NEW YORK • LONDON
AMSTERDAM • PARIS • SYDNEY • HAMBURG
STOCKHOLM • ATHENS • TOKYO • MILAN • MADRID
PRAGUE • WARSAW • BUDAPEST • AUCKLAND

To all the people who work with homeless animals,
with special thanks to the Westerly, R.I., dog shelter
for Charlie, to "Kissypet" in Missouri for Pookie
and to the "Hearts United for Animals" shelter in
Nebraska for Keely. Thanks for rescuing the best
four-legged friends a writer ever had.

ISBN 0-373-25902-6

BLAME IT ON COWBOYS

Copyright © 2000 by Kristine Rolofson.

This edition published by arrangement with Harlequin Books S.A.

Visit us at www.eHarlequin.com

Printed in U.S.A.

1

"I'M GETTING MARRIED."

Conversation around the card table of the Dead Horse ranch suddenly came to a screeching halt. Dusty opened his mouth and didn't close it. Marty's fingers froze on the pile of poker chips he'd just stacked into a neat pile, and Roy stopped dealing the cards. When Old Shorty swallowed his beer too fast and choked, Jake reached over and slapped him twice between the shoulder blades before turning to stare at his boss. "You want to repeat that?"

"I'm getting married." The young man grinned. He leaned back in his chair and put his hands behind his head. "I guess I surprised you all, huh?"

Jake, the only one capable of speech, wasn't impressed. "This is some kind of joke, right?"

"No, sir. No way. Don't you want to know who I'm marrying?"

Four of the men nodded, so Bobby continued. "Amy Lou Comstock, from back East." He frowned, the way he did when he was thinking hard. "She lives in that little state, Rhode Island, but went to school in Colorado."

"An Eastern girl, huh? Makes sense," Shorty mumbled. "Since none of the local gals will have anything to do with you. You've just about broken all their hearts."

"I don't know about that," Dusty interjected. "Jessie left a message for him the other day, and the Wynette twins were hanging around the barns all weekend."

"They could've been there to see me." Marty, who spent most of his days and half of his nights trying to keep up with Bobby, tapped his poker chips. "I've made enough money tonight to take 'em both to the movies Sunday night."

Jake took a long drink of beer and set the bottle on the table before he spoke. After all, he didn't want to get his hopes up again. Getting Bobby to settle down had been a futile exercise for many a year now. The kid acted more like fifteen than twenty-five; his unending energy made Jake feel a lot older than thirty-five. More like fifty, he figured. And that was on a *good* day. "Well, that's interesting news," he drawled, hoping they all hadn't just been sucked into one of Bobby's pranks. "When's the wedding?"

The young man hesitated, making Jake's stomach tighten. "I'm trying for this summer, soon as I can, but Amy Lou said she wants her aunt to meet me first."

"Her aunt," Shorty repeated, nodding approvingly. "So she's a family kind of gal. That's good."

"Yep," the boy agreed. "I guess. If the old aunt likes me."

"You can sweet-talk the auntie," Marty declared. "Piece of cake for a charmer like you."

Jake wasn't so sure. Three cooks in the past two years had quit, saying they were "decent women" who weren't going to put up with Bobby's shenanigans one minute more. The main house, never much to look at, now seemed downright decrepit. What made Bobby think this place was ready to impress a couple of city women? It was clearly time to find out exactly what was going on. Jake leaned forward and looked the boy in the eye. "Where'd you meet a girl from Rhode Island? And how come we've never heard of her?"

"It's a long story." Bobby grinned and grabbed a handful of taco chips from the ripped bag by his elbow. He looked at his attentive audience. "You sure you wouldn't rather play poker?"

Roy put the deck of cards down. "I'd sure rather try to win a hand or two, but I guess everyone else can't mind their own business," he grumbled. "Just let me know when you want me to start dealing again."

"Don't pay any attention to him," Marty said. "Does this Amy Lou have a sister?"

"No." Bobby finished off the chips and wiped his hands on his jeans. "Just the aunt."

"Damn." He looked up hopefully. "How old's the aunt?"

The future groom shrugged. "Amy said she was pretty old. She is—was—a teacher."

"Teachers scare the heck out of me."

Jake was running out of patience. "Get back to how you met this girl," he ordered.

"Remember when I went to deliver horses to the McAllisters in April?"

Jake remembered. Bobby had stayed for four weeks and missed the end of a grueling calving season.

"They had company," Bobby continued. "The older daughter's college roommates." He picked up his beer. "From Colorado."

"Does she go to school in Boston or Colorado?" Jake still didn't believe this latest announcement. Leave it to Bobby to play a prank like this.

"Transferred to Colorado last year," he said. "Or something like that. I didn't pay much attention to that part of the conversation, if you know what I mean." He winked at Marty.

"You have all the luck," Marty grumbled. "I just can't figure it out."

Bobby shrugged. "Just comes naturally, I guess."

"What's natural is that load of bull you keep coming up with," Roy said. "Are we gonna play cards or not?"

"It was love at first sight," the kid declared. "Hit

me just like when lightning hit that old cottonwood
a few years ago. You know, the one down by the
creek in the west pasture where—"

"Love," Shorty interrupted, because everyone interrupted Bobby when he started off on one of his
tangents. "Love can sure get a man in trouble pretty
damn fast. You sure you know what you're doing,
son?"

"Sure I'm sure." He glanced toward Jake, and his
smile faltered. "Don't look so serious, Jake. I'm the
one getting married, not you."

"And it's a good thing, too," Jake replied. "Considering I wouldn't want to be the one having to figure out how to get this old place ready for company.
Especially *female* company," he added, hoping to
make the damn kid squirm a little.

"Yeah?" Bobby looked pretty relaxed.

"Yeah," Jake said. "If you want to get married—"
and Jake sure hoped the boy did "—then we've got
to figure out a few things. Like cleaning. And cooking. And what you're going to do with Gus. And
how you're gonna keep the Wynette girls out of the
barn."

"And how to keep Amy's old auntie from cramp-
ing my style."

Jake frowned. "You're not going to...well, you
know what you're not going to do here on the home
place."

"Yeah, I know." But he didn't look thrilled about

it, making Jake wonder if the boy had already se-
duced his Amy Lou. The sooner he got Bobby married, the sooner Jake could stop worrying about the
boy getting someone in trouble. There would be no
more unwanted kids at the Dead Horse, not as long
as Jake was in charge.

"Well, then, we need a plan."

"We could plan to play a few more hands of
poker, that's what we could do." Roy picked up the
cards and started dealing where he'd left off. "It's
not even nine o'clock."

"Good idea," Bobby said, tossing a red chip into
the center of the table. "Let's make this interesting,
okay?"

Everyone but Jake eagerly agreed.

Bobby picked up his cards, but before he looked
at them he winked at Jake and said, "Loser gets the
aunt."

Jake shook his head. "Gets the aunt? What the
hell does that mean?"

"She's gonna need a chaperone, someone to show
her the ranch and fix her tea and help her in and out
of the truck and all that kind of stuff."

"Aw, Bobby," Roy moaned as he finished dealing
the cards. "I thought we was gonna play cards, not
talk about women any more."

His boss ignored him and tossed a blue chip into
the center of the table. "Who's in?"

"We all are. Now," Jake added, putting the "old

auntie" out of his mind. "And we're only playing till nine, because we've got calves to brand first thing in the morning."

"No problem," Bobby assured him, picking up his cards and smiling at what he saw. "No way I'll hafta take care of Auntie with a good hand like this."

Dusty glared at him. "You're bluffing. Again."

"You'll just have to wait and see," the young man drawled. He picked up a red chip and tossed it into the pile. "My turn to open."

Jake glanced at his cards, but his mind wasn't on poker, that was for sure. He was thinking of Bobby growing up and getting married. Settling down. Becoming a responsible member of the community. Which deserved a cold beer if anything did. "Hand me another one of those," he told Dusty, whose chair was next to the cooler stuffed with ice, beer and cans of sugar-free iced tea, because Roy was diabetic and Shorty only drank on Saturday nights.

"I thought we were only playing till nine," Bobby teased as he passed the can of beer to Jake.

"I'll drink it fast," he promised, still eyeing the younger man. "You know what getting married means, don't you? No more women. Plural."

"Yes, sir," he said. "There's only one woman for me now."

Jake wished he could believe it. He didn't dare imagine how simple life would be. He folded his cards and opened the beer. "I'm out," he said, unwilling to risk any money on a hand with an eight high. "No use wasting money. Not when Bobby's so pleased with himself."

Besides, if this news was true, his good luck was just beginning.

ELIZABETH COMSTOCK eyed the tiny bundle of fur that was asleep in the middle of her kitchen floor. Snoring softly, the six-pound Shih Tzu lay curled up in his bed and appeared completely oblivious to the two women who watched him. "I don't know what I'm going to do with him."

"He loves you," Amy replied, and gave her aunt a bright smile.

"He doesn't know any better," Elizabeth pointed out. "He's not very bright."

Amy sat down on the white tile and stroked the dog's back. "When I get married I'm going to have big dogs."

"Could we stop talking about marriage for a few minutes?" Elizabeth looked at her watch. She had expected to have the car packed and the condo closed up by one, in time to avoid rush hour traffic on Interstate 195. Rhode Island's major highways took a beating during the summer season, and it was best to avoid commuter traffic along with the Friday afternoon rush to the Cape. "I'm running late. Can you take him out for me?"

"Sure. I'm all packed, too."

"You're determined to go to Texas, even after everything I've said—'"

"I don't know why not," Amy grumbled. "I'm twenty-one and all grown up."

"Of course you are," Elizabeth fibbed. "But that doesn't necessarily mean you're ready for marriage." And talking didn't necessarily mean that her niece would listen to her advice, either.

"I'm in love. Don't you believe me?"

Elizabeth pulled the garbage can over to the refrigerator. She opened the door and started tossing perishables into the plastic liner. "I believed you when you wanted to elope with your English professor, the one who said you had a gift for poetry."

"But—"

"And I believed you when you dropped out of school to study art in Italy with—what was his name?"

"Vincenzo."

"And then there was that television director who said you'd be perfect for *Baywatch*."

"I had a part—"

"You screamed at a jellyfish in a crowd scene." She eyed a chunk of mozzarella cheese, then tucked it into the overcrowded freezer. One of these days, she promised herself, she would clean out the freezer and make a casserole.

Amy shrugged. "I don't think Hollywood appreciated me. Except for the scream, I mean. I'll bet I could have done horror flicks."

"And this cowboy *does* appreciate you?"

"He's cute. And funny. And he looks sooooo good in jeans." Amy sighed.

"A necessary requirement for a husband, I'm sure."

"You know what they say about cowboys, don't you?"

"No, and I don't want to." Elizabeth didn't want to know anything more about cowboys. She wanted to go to Cape Cod and shop for antiques and read mystery novels and wear flowered sundresses that made her feel cool and summery. She wanted to dunk chunks of lobster in melted butter and sip icy cold wine. "I've bought sunscreen and a new bathing suit and I'm all set to open up the beach house—"

"I'd like you to meet my future husband," Amy said. "Since you're my only living relative and everything."

Which, of course, was the problem. Amy had been hers for the past five and a half years, ever since her mother died. And Elizabeth had taken her role of guardian seriously. Too seriously, Amy insisted now that she was twenty-one. But Amy was the kind of girl who got herself in the strangest predicaments and forever needed rescuing.

"Come on, Auntie B," Amy said, picking up the

little dog and cradling him in her lap. "Pookie can come, too."

"He'll have to," Elizabeth murmured. "I can't imagine putting him in a kennel."

"Then you're saying you'll go with me?"

"No way. The last time I got you out of trouble, I ended up snowed in—" she stopped, remembering that weekend in Chicago.

"You can't blame the blizzard on me."

No, Elizabeth thought. And she couldn't blame what happened that night on anyone but herself. "Why can't you just go back to college and date normal boys?"

"Bobby's normal, for a Texan. He owns a ranch," Amy explained. "And he wants me—us—to see it."

"Last fall all you wanted was to go back to college. Now you want to go to Texas and see a ranch and someone named Bobby who told you he owned a ranch. How do you know he's telling the truth?"

Amy shrugged. "The McAllisters said he owned one of the biggest operations in Texas. Or the county. Or something. You'll like him."

No, she wouldn't. And even if she did, Amy was too young to get married. "You're too young to get married," Elizabeth said out loud, shutting the refrigerator. She made the mistake of glancing toward her niece, whose eyes looked as if they'd filled with tears. "Don't do this to me, Amy."

"You can go to the beach after you meet him."

"Texas is a long way from Cape Cod," she said, but Elizabeth knew she'd let herself be talked into falling in with Amy's plan.

"You'll only have to stay a little while. And you have all summer on the beach, till school starts." Amy stood and tucked the sleepy Pookie against her chest. "Please? I already bought our tickets."

"The Atlantic Ocean versus hot, dry Texas," Elizabeth muttered, already knowing what her decision would be. "Gee, what a choice."

"Come on, Auntie B. It'll be fun."

No, it wouldn't, Elizabeth knew, tying the garbage bag shut. Keeping Amy out of trouble never was.

"I LOOKED in the paper, Jake. There's a quilt show in Beauville next weekend."

"A quilt show," Jake repeated, eyeing his boss with a decided lack of enthusiasm. Trust Bobby to come up with something like this. "What the hell am I supposed to do while this old lady looks at quilts?"

The young man fidgeted with his hat, smoothed his hair and replaced his Stetson so that his eyes were shaded against the afternoon sun. "Might not be so bad," he said, but he didn't meet Jake's gaze. "Colorful, even."

"I was thinking about antiques," Jake suggested. "Those older ladies like all that old stuff."

Bobby brightened. "Yeah, like doilies and lace, stuff like that. Good idea. Cards, too," he added. "Gus told me his mother used to like canasta and bridge."

"I can see I'm going to be busy driving around Texas." Jake rested one booted foot on the bottom rail of the corral and turned to look at the three young mares prancing idly inside. "What about them?"

"I'll do it soon. This week." Bobby shoved his hands in the pockets of his jeans and glanced toward the horses. "Training them mares will impress the hell out of Amy Lou."

"Yeah, I suppose it will."

"She likes cowboys," he announced proudly.

Jake hid a sigh. *Don't they all.* Women had been trailing after Bobby before he was old enough to figure out why.

"And you know, I look damn good on a horse."

Jake didn't think Bobby expected a coherent reply.

"You'll like her."

Jake nodded. He'd worship the ground she walked on if Bobby turned into a responsible husband and rancher.

"And her auntie can't be so bad."

The older man started to point out that young women and old women could be all sorts of trouble, but then he figured he'd save his breath. Jake had put in a full day's work, and what energy he had left would be spent eating supper. What they needed— what *he* needed—was a nice domestic woman, the kind of woman who smelled like cinnamon and vanilla. The kind of woman who wouldn't yell too much about dirt being tracked in on her clean kitchen floor, who'd welcome a man into her bed each night without acting like she was doing him a big favor.

Unfortunately, he didn't know any women like that around here, under the age of forty, anyway. Which brought him back to their subject. "Can this Amy Lou cook?"

Bobby shrugged. "I dunno."

Not a good sign, but Jake remained calm. "Has she ever lived in the country or ridden a horse?"

"I doubt it, but what the hell. She can learn." Bobby sighed. "Gee, Jake, I thought you'd be happy I was finally getting married."

Happy? Jake wanted to dance the two-step down the drive and back again. He wanted to pass out cigars and open that bottle of whiskey he'd been saving. Never mind that he didn't smoke and he rarely drank anything stronger than beer, forget that he had two left feet and there wasn't a woman in sight. But Bobby needed to be practical. What was a city woman going to think of spending the rest of her life on a cattle ranch? "Let's put it this way, kid. I'll believe it when I see it."

"You'll see it tonight," the boy promised, checking his watch. "I'll be heading to the airport pretty quick."

"You feeding them before you bring them back here, I hope?" The airport was a four-hour round trip, which would put them all back here at seven unless Bobby stopped at a restaurant.

"Sure." The kid grinned. "You're worried about the food?"

"I was." Until Jake had hired Marty's mother to get some groceries and cook the evening meal each night. He'd had to double the usual wage and promise Mrs. Martin that there'd be "no shenanigans." Jake wasn't real clear about the definition of shenanigans, but he'd assured the temporary cook that Bobby's so-called fiancée was bringing her maiden aunt along to chaperone. "But I've got it figured out. How long do you think they're staying?"

Bobby grinned and tilted his hat low on his forehead. "Until I get my way, of course."

Jake wished him all the luck in the world. And told him so. Because what this place needed was a woman's touch. What the world needed was Bobby Calhoun to tie the knot and stay home at night.

"I'm glad you're settling down," Jake said, wondering if Bobby knew how fervently he wished for a little peace and quiet.

"Yeah." He grinned. "Did I tell you she was on *Baywatch?*"

"Three or four times," Jake replied, which meant she was blond with huge breasts, and nothing unusual in Texas. Jake figured it had something to do with the weather.

Bobby pulled a crumpled piece of paper from his shirt pocket. "I got some more ideas last night," he said, handing it to Jake. "To keep the auntie out of the way."

Jake smoothed the paper and squinted at the scrawled words. "Looking at flowers," he read aloud. "Movies. Shopping." He looked toward Bobby. "How am I supposed to get any work done?"

"We'll manage."

"Yeah, right," Jake mumbled, folding the paper carefully before tucking it into his back pocket. "You'll have to take up the slack."

"Amy will help. She's looking forward to it."

Jake tried to picture Amy Lou Comstock, the college-girl *Baywatch* babe, eating a mouthful of Texas dust. "Maybe you should go easy on her."

Bobby shook his head. "Nope. We talked about it, and she knows this ranch is part of the deal."

"The deal," Jake repeated.

"You know, the getting married and all that. Besides," the boy added, "she said she always wanted to live on a ranch. And she always wanted to meet a cowboy."

"How about that," Jake drawled, hoping that

Amy Lou wouldn't run screaming from Texas the first time she saw a rattlesnake.

"I'd better get going. Next time you see me, I'll be holding the hand of my fee-ahn-say," he declared, mimicking Shorty's pronunciation.

"I can't wait," Jake said, meaning the words. "I hope she'll be real happy here."

"Yeah?"

"Yeah."

Bobby shoved his hands in his pockets again and rocked nervously on his heels. "You talked to the guys about swearing and scratching and spitting in front of the ladies?"

Jake hid a smile. "Yeah."

"Good. I wouldn't want to give her the wrong impression, like we're crude or anything."

"No."

"Guess I'd better get going." Bobby had turned pale, like he'd looked when he was twelve the afternoon he'd smoked his first cigar.

"Yeah. Good luck." Jake watched Bobby cross the field and head toward the garage before he walked across the yard to his own home.

The small yellow house with the side porch belonged to Jake. At least, that's where he hung his hat at night and kept his clean clothes. It needed fresh paint and the middle porch step squeaked, but nothing to complain about, that was for sure. He worked a small spread forty miles northwest of the

Dead Horse, on a nice-size piece of adjoining land the old man had left him, but for the time being he lived close to Bobby. Old man Calhoun had known what he was doing, though no one in the county ever called R.J. Calhoun a fool, not to his face and not behind his back.

"Reckless," the old man had muttered, leaving the gravesite of his son and daughter-in-law. Jake had only been eighteen at the time, but he'd lived at the Dead Horse for as long as he could remember, because his mother had been R.J.'s devoted housekeeper. And he'd been following R.J. around since he was old enough to wear boots and open the kitchen door without help. "We'll have to take good care of the boy, you and me."

"Yes, sir." Jake had straightened his shoulders and clapped young Bobby on the shoulders to guide him back to the waiting limousine.

And that had been that, Jake remembered, moving toward the yellow house. R.J. was gone twenty-two months later, and the next thirteen years had passed by fast, hurried by hard work and long days and the dual responsibilities of being both foreman and guardian to a kid whose middle name was Trouble.

Jake would clean up, fix himself a couple of roast beef sandwiches and work on the accounts until Bobby returned with the women. Maybe he'd even study this list and come up with some ideas of his own.

And he'd damn well make sure that old Auntie Bea *loved* Texas by the time he was through with her.

2

"THE TROUBLE with Aunt Elizabeth," Amy told Bobby on the telephone at the airport, "is that she's never been in love."

"That's real sad," Bobby declared, sounding as if it was the worst news he'd ever had.

"Or if she has she certainly hasn't talked about it." Which meant it hadn't worked out, Amy assumed. If there had been any grand passion in her aunt's past then Amy would have known about it, because she and her aunt were so close. And everyone knew the only happy ending was a walk down the aisle. Besides, why wouldn't any man fall in love with her aunt? She was pretty and smart, though maybe a little on the prudish side.

"How long is she gonna stay?"

"I don't know. I just wanted the two of you to meet each other before—" Amy hesitated and shifted her cell phone to her other ear. She hadn't said she'd marry him yet. Not until Aunt B met him.

"Before you agree to marry me?" Bobby finished the sentence for her. "Honey, just say yes now and

I'll call the justice of the peace out to the ranch and we'll do it up right."

"Soon," she promised. Amy hadn't thought much beyond the wedding itself. She pictured herself changing out of her flowing Victorian-style white gown into jeans and riding a palomino horse alongside Bobby. Together they would do whatever ranchers did, and they would have picnics and make love on faded quilts in the middle of a prairie covered with wildflowers. "I can't wait to see you."

"Well, honey, you're gonna get your wish this afternoon. I sure have missed you."

"Mmm," she said, thinking of her aunt again. "I don't think Aunt B will stay long. She has a beach house on the Cape."

"What cape?"

"Cape Cod. Massachusetts. It's right on the ocean," Amy explained, remembering that Texas was a long way from New England. "It might even be a good place for our honeymoon." Her fantasies switched from quilts on the prairie to swimming naked in the moonlight, the ocean pounding their naked bodies against each other until—

"I'm not much for oceans, Amy Lou." Her almost-fiancé cleared his throat self-consciously. "Truth is, I don't even like boats."

"That's okay. It was just a thought. I'm sure Aunt B will head back there right after we—*if* we get married. I hate to think of her alone, though. Maybe she'll meet someone on the beach this summer."

"It's probably a little late for her now, isn't it?"

"I guess." She sighed. It was all so tragic somehow. Why couldn't everyone be as happy as she and Bobby Calhoun? She was sure her aunt would love him, absolutely positive that everything would work out just perfectly.

ELIZABETH rested her head against the blue leather seat of the extra-wide Cadillac and closed her eyes. Bobby and Amy, chattering in the front seat while the young cowboy drove at death-defying speeds along the empty highway, seemed to have forgotten they weren't alone.

She began to get sleepy, so Elizabeth forced herself to open her eyes to check on her niece. Amy's perfect, smiling profile faced her cowboy's, who took his gaze off the road much too often for Elizabeth's peace of mind. They couldn't take their eyes off each other, and Bobby drove with one hand on the wheel because the other stretched along the back of the seat and caressed Amy's bare shoulder.

Ah, love. Was this how it worked? And would she ever find out for herself or was she destined to turn into an old lady, complaining about the younger generation's driving speeds while sitting in the back seat alone? Well, not alone, exactly. Pookie sat snuggled beside her, in his typical state of contentment with wherever he happened to be, pretty mild company for a thirty-year-old chaperone relegated to the tail end of a car the size of a dining room.

No one warned her that the ranch was hours away from the Dallas-Fort Worth airport. Amy's cowboy had been handsome and young and enthusiastic, although he seemed surprised when Amy introduced her to him. He'd mumbled something neither woman could hear, but he'd hurried to remove his Stetson, then shook her hand with gusto, and a big grin spread across his face.

Elizabeth figured that if he'd known that Aunt B meant to take still-single Amy home to New England as soon as humanly possible, he probably wouldn't have looked so pleased.

"Are we there yet?" Amy sounded as excited as a five-year-old.

"Yep, almost." The car picked up speed, making Elizabeth grip the door handle with one hand and Pookie with the other.

"Mr. Calhoun?" she called.

"Yes, ma'am?"

"If you're going to drive at the speed of light, would you mind putting both hands on the steering wheel?"

"Yes, ma'am," he said, hurrying to move his arm. "I mean, no, ma'am, I don't mind at all." He dared to glance behind him, to give Elizabeth what he ob- viously thought was a manly, reassuring look.

"And please keep your eyes on the road," Eliza- beth said, in her most pleasant I-mean-business voice. It was the voice that halted rebellious teen- agers in their tracks, and she knew its power.

What she didn't know was how she was going to get back to the airport on Monday, but hijacking the Cadillac and driving it herself was not out of the realm of possibility. Pookie licked her hand, so she scratched his ears and watched him stretch with delight.

"We work hard and drive fast," she heard Bobby tell her niece. "I guess it takes some getting used to if you're not from around here."

"I'll get used to it," Amy promised, and Elizabeth wondered if it would be possible to be on the beach on Tuesday as if this visit to Texas had never hap- pened. Which book would she read first—the new Sandra Brown or the latest Jeffrey Deaver? She would buy some rum for frozen daiquiris and she would invite the couple next door over for dinner one night next weekend. Elizabeth closed her eyes and pretended she was in her chaise longue facing the ocean and didn't wake up until the car jolted to a stop.

"This is it, honey," Bobby said, and Elizabeth opened her eyes to see her niece being kissed. It was a brief embrace, however, because a giant brown dog leaped at the window and barked at Bobby, who immediately released Amy. "Hey, Gus!"

"Bobby?" Amy put her hand on his shoulder.

"Don't worry, honey," the cowboy said, opening the car door. "Get back, Gus. You're scaring the ladies, dammit!"

Elizabeth gripped Pookie a little tighter, determined to take care of everybody she'd inherited, even a six-pound bundle of hair. Her scatterbrained niece wouldn't last long here in *Gunsmoke* country, and Elizabeth didn't intend to let the child make another crazy mistake.

HE WOULDN'T be human if he wasn't curious. Or so Jake told himself, heading toward the house right after he'd seen the car along the road, dust billowing out from the tires as Bobby sped home with his intended bride.

No, Jake thought, slapping the dirt off his work gloves by hitting them on a fence post. It was time to meet this young lady, time to make a good impression on her aunt, time to pray that this would all work out and he, Jake, could move into his own home, on his own ranch, and start living his own life. He would be the best damn escort in Texas, if that's what it took.

He was within thirty yards of the Cadillac when he saw Bobby introducing Gus to a fair-haired young woman he guessed was the Comstock girl.

Then the car door opened to reveal another woman in the process of getting out of the car, awkward because her arms were loaded with jackets and bags. She wore something tan and short—hell, he could see half of her thighs but he wasn't complaining—and sandals with heels finished off a damn good-looking set of legs. He couldn't see her face, because she had turned around to talk to the younger woman, but he saw gold-streaked chestnut hair that fell to her bare shoulders.

She was clearly not the old-lady aunt. Jake continued to stride toward them, worried that the older woman was still in the car, possibly afraid of the dog or waiting for someone to help her out.

"Jake! Come on over here and meet everyone," Bobby called, waving one arm in his direction while hanging on to the girlfriend with the other.

Gus, standing on his hind legs, was busy jumping on the other woman, who freed one arm to bat him away. "Get down," he heard her command, and the dog did exactly that with his tail between his legs as he sought shelter behind Bobby.

She glanced in Jake's direction, her eyes hidden by sunglasses too large for her face, and continued to stare at him as he approached the car. He knew he should have cleaned up before they got here, but he'd gotten caught up with the horses longer than he'd planned.

"Here's Amy Lou," Bobby announced, his arm

curled possessively around a petite blonde. "Amy, this is Jake Johnson, ranch foreman."

He'd never seen anyone less likely to be a ranch wife, Jake decided, shaking Amy's delicate hand. She was a pretty young woman, so he could see why Bobby was smitten with her. It wasn't his business if she looked more like a centerfold than a fiancée. "Welcome to the Dead Horse ranch," he said politely.

"Thanks. I'm really glad to be here."

"And this here's Amy's aunt," Bobby said, stifling a laugh as he gestured toward the woman in the short skirt. "Aunt Bea."

Jake turned to look at her. "Aunt Bea?"

"My aunt Elizabeth," Amy said. "Aunt B is just a nickname."

"Please call me Elizabeth," the woman said.

And then he knew. Or he thought he did. Jake narrowed his eyes and studied this aunt who wasn't an old lady and who wasn't at all what he expected. She was the right height, about five-seven. The right shape, with an unforgettable pair of long legs. She wore no wedding ring, and her fingers were long, the nails polished and perfect. The hair was lighter and longer, the mouth—

"Jake? You want to help me with the bags?"

"Sure." But he didn't turn away, even though Elizabeth followed Bobby to the back of the Cadillac. That's when Jake noticed that the jacket she held in her arms had brown hair, bulging eyes and a ponytail on top of its head "What the he—heck is that?"

Amy reached out and plucked the animal from her aunt's embrace. "This is Pookie. He's a Shih Tzu. Isn't he cute?"

And here he'd thought nothing could make him stop staring at Aunt Bea. "It's a dog?"

She cuddled the passive animal as if it was a baby while Gus ventured closer to have a sniff. "Sort of."

"Don't let Gus get near it," Jake warned, picking up the bags that Bobby deposited on the ground. "I'm not sure if he'd think it was something to eat or something to chase."

Amy held the dog higher in her arms, and the creature snuggled into her neck. "We'll be careful. We couldn't leave him in a kennel because he gets scared."

After seeing Elizabeth, Jake was a little scared himself. She had to be the same woman. If she would only take those sunglasses off so he could get a look at her face, then he would know. He stared at her again, but she gave him a quick smile and then ignored him.

"You'll have to excuse Jake," Bobby said, shutting the trunk. "We were expecting an, uh, older lady."

Elizabeth glanced at her niece. "How old?"

"*Really* old." Bobby grinned and picked up the last bag.

"I'm sure that's how Amy thinks of me," Elizabeth said. "I've taken care of her for years and I do my best to protect her from...trouble."

There was a warning in those words, Jake realized, as he followed the women to the main house. Maybe Bobby had better not count his chickens before they said, "I do."

"You're gonna have a real nice time," Bobby said, leading the way as if he didn't have a care in the world. "Everyone likes the Dead Horse. And Beauville is a real nice town, too, just forty miles from here, real close."

"I love it already," Amy declared.

Jake would have given a lot to know what Aunt Elizabeth was thinking. And if she was the same woman he'd made love to last February.

THERE WERE TIMES when life wasn't fair, Elizabeth decided. Times when fate played nasty, sneaky, mean little tricks on people who most certainly did not deserve it. Such as now, when she was only trying to be a good aunt.

Elizabeth had not expected to run into this particular man. Not here. Not now. Not ever. She wondered if she was blushing. Elizabeth managed to stride across the dusty yard to Bobby Calhoun's house without turning and running to the Cadillac to make a quick escape back to the airport.

She admired the enormous, air-conditioned

kitchen, greeted an unhappy-looking housekeeper and remembered to thank Bobby for his hospitality. She did not meet the questioning gaze of Jake Johnson. Instead she asked where Pookie could be, hoping he wasn't getting in the way of the ranch animals. And all the time she was praying to all the gods in the heavens that Jake the Cowboy wouldn't recognize her.

"That's a dog?" Mrs. Martin asked. "He isn't going to make a mess on my clean floors, is he?"

Elizabeth certainly hoped not, but with Pookie there were no guarantees. "We'll watch him very carefully." It was the best she could come up with.

"He's not very smart," Amy explained, turning the dog to face Mrs. Martin. "But he loves to be held. And he's very sweet."

"Hmmph." It was all the stocky woman said, removing her apron to hang it on a hook by the door. "There's a chicken casserole in the oven in case you get hungry later on," she told Bobby. "Iced tea's in the fridge and there's fruit salad, too. Jake said you were going to stop on the way and eat, but Bobby here is always hungry."

"Thank you," Elizabeth said. "It smells wonderful."

The woman looked back at both of them and frowned. "I was told there'd be no shenanigans going on around here."

"Me, too." Elizabeth knew exactly what the

woman meant. "And there certainly won't be," she answered.

"Now, Mrs. Martin," Bobby said, holding open the kitchen door for her to leave. "Amy Lou's my fiancée, and Miss, uh, Comstock is her chaperone. Don't you worry about anything."

"I'll worry until you and Marty settle down and quit getting into jackpots," she muttered, going out the door. "There's a chocolate cake for dessert, but make sure you save some for the others."

"I will," Bobby promised, and when she was gone he turned to grin at his guests. "Don't pay any attention to Mrs. Martin. She's known me all my life."

"Who's Marty?" Amy asked.

"One of my best friends. He works here." Bobby went over to the refrigerator and opened the door. "What would you like to drink, ladies? Beer? Iced tea? Something stronger?"

"Beer," Amy declared, though Elizabeth had never seen her drink anything other than white wine.

"Nothing for me, thanks," Elizabeth said, hoping that Jake would leave the house and return to wherever he came from. "Would you mind if I unpacked?"

Bobby grinned, probably at the thought of having Amy all to himself for a few minutes while the chaperone disappeared. "No, ma'am. We've got the rooms all fixed up, thanks to Mrs. Martin."

Jake picked up the bags he'd left by the back door. "I'll show you where you're sleeping while Bobby fixes drinks." He walked over to a door and peered into another room. "Mrs. Martin has the table all set for dinner." He turned to Elizabeth, who felt perspiration trickle down her back. "Would you like to follow me, Ms. Comstock?"

"Of course," she managed to reply, and even made her voice sound remote and cool. She turned to her niece. "Amy?"

"I'll be along in a minute." Amy rearranged Pookie in her arms. "Bobby's going to show me where Pook can go do his business."

And of course that couldn't wait, not with a dog whose bladder was the size of a dime. "Oh. Fine."

But nothing was fine, Elizabeth thought, following the tall cowboy out of the kitchen. He didn't remember her, she told herself, hoping for some kind of comfort in the thought. He must have had lots of sex in lots of hotel rooms during lots of blizzards. And they had exchanged names, but she'd told him she was Beth. She'd never thought his name, Jake Johnson, was real. Who would do that?

Well, someone you thought you'd never see again, of course.

He led her past an old-fashioned dining room, down a wide hall and around a corner to a narrow set of stairs. "This is the back way," he said. "There's a front staircase off the living room, but no one uses it. But you can if you want."

She didn't say a word. And she didn't remove her sunglasses, despite the darkness of the staircase as they made their way upstairs. They stood at the end of a hall that smelled inviting, whose wood floors gleamed with fresh polish underneath dust-free pastel scatter rugs.

"You're here on the right," Jake said, pushing open a door with his elbow. She followed him into a dimly lit room, the window shades drawn against the late afternoon sun. "It's small," he said, "but you have your own bathroom. We thought you'd like privacy."

She felt like an idiot with her sunglasses still on, so she slipped them off and held onto them as casually as she could manage and turned away to admire the yellow-striped wallpaper and pine dresser. She glanced at the double bed, simply made with white sheets, a blue and yellow flowered comforter folded at one end, and then dared to look at Jake. She'd pretend he was a stranger, no matter if he said otherwise. "It's lovely. And where is Amy sleeping?"

"Across the hall. The upstairs hasn't been used for years, so make yourself comfortable." He dropped her bags at the foot of the bed.

Meaning Amy's true love of the month slept

downstairs and wouldn't be making nocturnal visits.

"Thank you." So he didn't recognize her, she decided, despite the fact that he was gazing at her and frowning. "I guess I'm not exactly what you expected. How old was I supposed to be?"

He almost smiled, but something stopped him. "About ninety. Have we met before?"

"I doubt it."

The man had the nerve to step closer to her. "Are you sure?"

"Of course." She held his gaze for as long as she dared, then pretended to admire the room again.

"Do you go to Chicago often?"

"Chicago?" Elizabeth edged toward the bathroom door. When in doubt, hide. "No. I teach algebra at—"

"Then you don't travel," he interrupted, as if he didn't want to hear anything other than her vacation plans.

"Not very often. I spend summers in Massachusetts," she declared, then shot him a bright smile. "Mr. Johnson, would you mind excusing me? I'd like to freshen up."

"No problem. I'll go get the rest of the bags."

"You don't have to wait on us. We can—"

"You don't understand, lady," the man said.

She hadn't forgotten how handsome he was, not in the months since she'd last seen him sprawled naked in the hotel bed. He'd hogged the covers, but she'd managed to snuggle against his back and stay warm. Very warm.

"Understand what?" Blue eyes, dark hair, broad shoulders and a very stubborn chin were not things she could forget easily, especially since those shoulders had pinned her very nicely to a mattress.

"My job is to show you around, take you places, see that you're happy."

"That's ridiculous. I certainly don't need—"

"Doesn't matter what you need," Jake declared. "I'm yours," he said, smiling slightly as he gazed directly into her eyes. "For as long as you're here."

3

ELIZABETH WATCHED Jake leave the room and thought about faking a killer headache that would keep her in bed until morning. She would even be glad to have an *authentic* killer headache, since anything would be better than having another conversation with Jake Johnson, especially one that ended with "I'm yours."

She blamed her wobbly legs on jet lag, her racing heart on drinking strongly brewed coffee on the flight and refused to believe that one man could turn her into a shaky-kneed coward with just one look.

Elizabeth went into the bathroom and washed her hands of Texas dust and Pookie hair before squaring her shoulders and leaving the cozy bedroom. She knew she certainly couldn't leave Amy alone with her boyfriend. He'd have her niece out of her clothes and flat on her back within fifteen minutes of the first kiss. Elizabeth blushed to think she knew about that from experience.

She peeked into the room across the hall before descending the narrow staircase. The house was nice enough, and it seemed that Bobby had been telling the truth about owning a cattle ranch, but ranching didn't seem like the most secure way to make a living. Then again, better than Hollywood directors or Paris artists. Amy had a knack of attracting unusual people.

The latest candidate met Elizabeth at the bottom of the stairs, his buffalo-size dog at his heels.

"Is your room all right?" Bobby looked frightened of her, which made Elizabeth almost feel sorry for him.

"It's lovely," she said, eyeing Gus. "Please move," she ordered, and the animal hid behind Bobby and allowed Elizabeth to step into the hall. "Where's Amy?"

The young man shot a worried glance at his dog, whose tail was between his legs. "She's outside with, uh, the Pookie dog, and Gus was making the little guy kinda nervous so I thought I'd bring the rest of her stuff upstairs. How'd you do that?"

"Do what?"

"Get Gus to mind. He's never been much for dog obedience, if you know what I mean. As a matter of fact, old Gus sort of does whatever he wants around—"

"Bobby! Hey, Bobby!" High-pitched voices called.

"Oh, Lord," the cowboy muttered, looking like he'd been caught stealing candy from babies. He dropped Amy's bags and turned reluctantly back to the kitchen.

"I think you have company," Elizabeth said, following him. And the company was female, which was interesting.

"The twins," he grumbled. "They won't leave me alone."

Somehow she doubted that the twins were under eighteen and suffering from a childish crush. She didn't want to see her niece hurt, but on the other hand, if the young cowboy had other women in his life, Elizabeth figured she and Amy could return to Dallas and catch a morning flight back to Providence. She'd have sand between her toes in twenty-four hours. It was a cheering thought.

"Hey, Bobby." Two identical blondes cooed. They stood side by side in front of the kitchen door and looked like cowgirl beauty queens. "Have you seen Marty anywhere around?"

"Uh, last time I saw him I think he was working on one of the bikes."

The twin teenagers—and Elizabeth didn't think they could be much older than eighteen—stared past Bobby to his guest. "Your company's here? Is this your girlfriend?"

"This is Amy Lou's auntie," Bobby said, giving Elizabeth a little push forward as if he thought he needed protection.

"Elizabeth Comstock," she said, filling in the introductions. "And you're obviously sisters."

"We're the Wynette twins," the one on the left said. "I'm Mandy."

"I'm Sandy," the other one added. "We're real sorry Bobby stopped runnin' around with us, but we got new outfits for the wedding."

"When's it gonna be, Bobby?"

"You'll be the first to know," he promised. "Me and Amy are still trying to figure that part out. So what are you two up to tonight?"

"Marty said he'd take us to the movies."

"If he's not too late."

Bobby hurried forward to usher them out the door. "Check in the shop," he said. "If he's not there holler at the bunkhouse and someone will tell you where he's at."

"Thanks, hon," one of them said, while the other girl waved to Elizabeth.

"See you later."

"Goodbye," Elizabeth called. "It was nice meeting you."

"Maybe I'd better go help them find Marty," Bobby said, hurrying out the door with Gus trotting at his heels. Elizabeth went to the window and watched them stroll toward a distant set of outbuildings. Boots, jeans, hats and checkered shirts worn by all three Texans made them look as if they belonged together. Why would her niece think she could become a rancher's wife and fit into this brown, dust-covered world?

"I LOVE IT HERE," Amy declared, rounding the corner of the house. The dog had done his business eventually, though the flat-faced animal had seemed perplexed by all the new smells. "It's just as I pictured a Texas ranch would be. Everything's so open and just like the movies."

"I'm real glad to hear it," Jake replied, holding Pookie under his arm like a football. Sure that Gus was waiting nearby to pounce on the canine intruder, Jake had decided to protect the Shih Tzu instead of carrying suitcases. He wasn't taking any chances. There was nothing surer to kill romance than the murder of a pet, especially if the killer was the guy's own dog. "I hope you'll be real happy here."

"Thanks." She shot him a grateful smile. "I hope everyone around here is as nice as you."

"We try."

"Bobby said you practically raised him."

"Well, I guess so, but—"

"And that you're like an uncle to him the way Elizabeth is an aunt to me."

He hoped she didn't expect him to start telling stories about the boy's childhood. He'd have to make up something real sweet and he wasn't good at thinking up things like that without a lot of advance warning. "Yeah, I guess you could say that. I worked for Bobby's grandfather."

"So you've lived here a long time?"

"All my life," he said, wondering what the girl was getting at.

"Bobby said that you're going to show my aunt around."

"Yes, ma'am, that's true."

Amy stopped in front of the kitchen door. "Can you try—I mean, *really* try—to make her like it here? I mean—" she stammered prettily "—that's why she came. I wanted her to see that I'd be happy."

"And you think you will be?" He thought she was awfully young.

Her smile was similar to her aunt's as she pushed open the door and stepped into the kitchen. "I'm sure of it. Do you believe in love at first sight?"

Jake saw Elizabeth by the window. He watched as she turned to meet his gaze, but she quickly looked toward Amy instead. "I'm not sure," he said slowly. "I've never been in love."

He didn't know why he'd admitted that, but it sure made Elizabeth look at him again.

"Never?" Amy sounded incredulous.

"Nope." He walked toward Elizabeth and handed her the dog. "Does he ever walk?"

"He walks," she said, managing to take Pookie without touching Jake's hands. "Sometimes. But he gets so confused about where he's going that it's simply easier to carry him or put him in his bed.''

"He has his own bed?" Jake asked.

"It's a little one," she said, a bit defensively.

"Do you take him everywhere?"

"I don't have much choice," Elizabeth said, petting the animal's head. "He wouldn't know what to do in a kennel."

Except sleep, Jake figured. "He doesn't look much like a dog. Not with that hair on top of his head like that."

"No." She took a step sideways as if she intended to flee the room.

"Are you *sure* we haven't met before?" Jake couldn't help himself. He knew exactly who she was. He didn't have to wonder any longer if she had a twin sister or a look-alike cousin who'd been stuck in O'Hare Airport last February. He didn't have to lie awake at night and wonder if he would ever find her again.

And what she'd do if he did.

Now he knew. The woman would look through him, ignore him, talk to him as if that one night had never happened, just like she wasn't the same woman he last saw naked and asleep, her soft breasts touching his forearm.

"I can't imagine how," she replied, not looking at him.

"I can."

"Where's Bobby?"

Elizabeth turned toward her niece and used the question as an excuse to step around Jake. "Some girls came looking for someone named Marty, who must be one of the other cowboys. They went off to find him."

"The twins were here?" Jake knew they wouldn't give up Bobby Calhoun easily.

"Yes."

"Okay," Amy said. "If you point me in the right direction I'm sure I can find him."

"I'll bet he'll be right back," Jack assured her, figuring this was no time for Amy and the Wynettes to meet each other.

"Over there," Elizabeth said, pointing out the window toward the bunkhouses. "I'm sure you can catch up with them."

The woman knew exactly what she was doing, damn her. Jake watched Amy hurry out of the kitchen, the door slamming behind her.

"You shouldn't have done that," he said.

"She has to find out sooner or later."

"Find out what?"

"That her new boyfriend has old girlfriends."

"Yeah," he agreed, studying those beautiful lips of hers. "Doesn't everyone?"

"I wouldn't know."

"Chicago," he said, taking a step closer to her. "O'Hare airport. February fourteenth."

"I really don't—"

He interrupted her as he moved within inches of her and the little dog she cradled in her arms. "You don't remember the snowstorm?

"Doesn't it usually snow in Chicago in February?"

"Nice try," he said, knowing damn well from the expression in those green eyes of hers that she knew exactly what he was talking about.

"I think you must have me confused with someone else." Holding the dog against her, she edged away from Jake toward the hall. "It happens to me all the time."

"How about that," he drawled, willing to let her off the hook for now. "Must be darned embarrassing at times."

"Yes."

Jake went over to a tall cupboard and opened it. He pulled out a bottle of wine and a bottle of whiskey. "I don't suppose the kid offered you a drink?"

"No, but I really don't—"

"Whiskey, wine, beer? What's your pleasure?"

"Nothing, thank you."

"Now, why would I think you like red wine?"

She didn't reply, but she looked surprised enough to please Jake. He helped himself to a generous amount of whiskey before suggesting she sit down and make herself comfortable. He then went to a cupboard and retrieved a bottle of wine.

"I really should find Amy," Elizabeth protested, glancing out the window toward the bunkhouses.

"She'll be fine. The twins won't let her or Bobby out of their sight, so you don't have to worry." Which was the truth. Those girls had arrived only to meet the fiancée and not to go to the movies with Marty. But if Bobby wanted a few minutes alone with Amy Lou, that was natural. And Jake didn't intend to get in the way of matrimonial progress.

After all, that was the whole point of this. Just because the future Mrs. Calhoun had brought along Jake's fantasy woman of last winter didn't mean that Bobby should get off track.

Jake decided to try to keep his questions to himself for now. Miss Elizabeth Comstock was going to be around for a while, and he was going to be her tour guide. He didn't have to rush his fences, so he changed the subject.

"Don't you get tired of holding him?"

That finally made the woman smile again. She reluctantly perched on a kitchen chair, plopped the dog in her lap and accepted a glass of wine from Jake. The hairy little guy looked like he was dead.

"It's ridiculous, I know," she admitted, "but I don't know what else to do with him. He gets scared when he's by himself and he's too old to learn anything new."

"I sometimes feel that way myself," he joked, hoping to see her smile once again.

"He's not really mine," she said. "He belonged to my aunt, and she spoiled him terribly."

"And you've got him now."

"You see, I inherit things," she explained. "Nieces, houses, rugs, silver...and even dogs." She took a sip of wine. "That's what happens when you're the oldest surviving member of the family."

"So you feel responsible for Amy."

"Of course."

"She's twenty-one," he pointed out. "Right?"

"Yes, but—"

"And an adult."

"Who still needs looking after," Elizabeth added, standing up and walking over to the window. "I wish they'd come back."

"They will," he assured her.

She stepped closer and peered outside. "Before or after they have sex?"

"What?"

Elizabeth pointed. "He's on top of her right now."

Jake was out the door within seconds, his hat on his head and his fists clenched at his sides as he strode across the yard. Sure enough, Bobby and Amy Lou were tangled together in the shade of the mechanics' shed. And they were laughing, not moaning in passion.

"What the hell are you two doing?" Jake kicked Bobby's booted foot. "Get up, before her aunt finds out where we keep the rifles."

Gus whined and wagged his tail, uncertain what was going on but ready to play.

"It's okay, Mr. Johnson," Amy said, laughing up at him as Bobby climbed to his feet. The young man held out his hand and tugged Amy up to stand beside him. She tugged her short dress over her thighs and blushed while Bobby reached down in the dirt to retrieve his hat. "It's all my fault, honest."

Jake turned to Bobby. "You've got something to say, I hope?"

The kid had the nerve to grin at him. "You've gotta blame Gus, Jake. Damn *darn* dog knocked Amy down and—"

"I screamed," she added. "Because I didn't know he was trying to play. I thought he was attacking me, so I grabbed Bobby and—"

"I fell," he said, still grinning as he dusted off his hat. "We just got all tangled up."

Jake didn't believe it for a minute, but then again, he'd never known Bobby to make love to anyone in the middle of the damn yard before.

Amy laughed again and tried to pet Gus, but he scurried away and hid behind Bobby as Elizabeth approached. "Sorry, Aunt B," she said, as her aunt hurried toward them. "I didn't mean to scare you."

"Gus knocked her down," Bobby said. "I told you he wasn't much for obeying anyone."

"I see," the aunt murmured, but Jake could tell

she didn't believe a word of it. She continued, "I'm sure you'd like to unpack."

Not an invitation, but a command, Jake noticed, though her niece didn't seem too concerned. The girl tucked her arm through Bobby's and smiled at him as if neither one of them was covered with dirt. Maybe he'd underestimated the little city gal, after all. Jake turned to Elizabeth, who still had that damn little dog tucked under her arm.

"Get away," Elizabeth said, and it took Jake a second to realize she was talking to Gus and not him. Not that he was about to pay any attention. In fact, he was damn sure he was going to get all the attention he wanted.

If he could ever get Elizabeth to admit she knew exactly who he was.

"ISN'T BOBBY adorable?" Amy knew her aunt didn't think any such thing, but she couldn't help teasing her. "Come on, Auntie B, admit that you didn't think the ranch would be this nice."

"I didn't think the ranch would be this nice," Elizabeth said obediently as she stood by the window.

Amy hurried to unpack so she could join Bobby downstairs. She'd no idea the ranch would be this big or that the life she'd envisioned for herself would be so wonderful in reality. "Aren't you glad you came?"

"For heaven's sake, Amy, this can't possibly

work," her aunt said, turning from the window and crossing her arms in front of her chest as she watched Amy unpack. Pookie, snuggled against the pillows piled high against an iron headboard, snored and wheezed.

"Why not?" Amy surveyed her collection of new silk underwear. Definitely fit for a bride. And a honeymoon.

"You barely know each other."

Amy smiled and stuffed the pastel underwear into the top drawer of an oak dresser. "We have our whole lives to do that."

"And that's another thing. You're both so...young."

She shrugged. "That doesn't matter."

Elizabeth closed her eyes briefly, as if praying for something. "Did you meet those twin girlfriends of his?"

"Former girlfriends," Amy countered, shoving the empty suitcase under the bed. "And yes, I thought they were really nice. Marty was happy to see them."

"Bobby wasn't."

"Aunt Elizabeth," Amy groaned, stepping around the bed to wrap her arms around the older woman's neck. "I do love you, but you really don't have any idea what it's like to be in love."

Elizabeth's shoulders shook, so Amy released her and began to stammer an apology.

"I didn't mean to make you feel bad—oh, you're laughing," she said, relieved. Amy wouldn't have hurt her serious, responsible, dedicated aunt for anything in the world.

"You treat me as if I'm one hundred years old," Elizabeth said, still smiling. "How do you know I don't have a man waiting for me on the Cape, some sex-crazed lobsterman counting the hours until I return to the dock and make his day?"

"Yeah, right," Amy said, rolling her eyes. "You'd tell me if you'd met someone."

"I would?"

"You wouldn't?"

Her aunt gave her that mind-your-own-business look, the one she usually ignored. But tonight she decided she'd better leave well enough alone. Aunt B was here, in Texas, about to put her seal of approval on Amy's marriage to a real cowboy. It wouldn't be smart to antagonize her.

"If you're finished, we should go downstairs and say good-night."

"Why?" Amy asked.

"It's after nine, honey. And it's been a long day."

"It's *barely* nine, Aunt B," Amy said, pausing in front of the dresser to brush her hair. She'd washed off the dust and changed into white shorts and a pink T-shirt, so she was ready to see her fiancé again. "It's still early and we thought we'd head to town for a while. Bobby's going to teach me how to two-step." She headed for the door. "Should we leave Pook up here?"

"I'll put him in his bed in my room," Elizabeth said, scooping the dog off the blue quilted bedspread.

"Bobby said Jake would come, too."

Her aunt spun around. "Would come where?"

"Dancing with us," Amy said, wondering if Aunt B was suffering from jet lag or something. "We're going to learn the two-step and drink beer in a real Texas bar."

"Amy, I just don't—"

"Aunt Elizabeth," Amy said, leading her aunt out of the bedroom and across the hall. "You really have to learn how to relax. Besides, Jake is nice-looking for an older guy. You could do worse."

"Yes," her aunt agreed in a strangled voice. "I could do worse."

"SHE'S BEAUTIFUL."

"She's trouble."

"Huh?"

"Not Amy," Jake said, hoping he was right about the young woman. He nodded toward Elizabeth, who looked very serious as she sipped a glass of wine and surveyed the wall of Western paintings that decorated the living room. He hoped Mrs. Martin had dusted the frames and polished the glass. Nobody used the room since Bobby had installed a large-screen television and a satellite dish in the main bunkhouse. "Elizabeth."

"Oh. The auntie." Bobby shrugged. "She's not so bad. I think she even likes me."

"How can you tell?" Genuinely interested in Bobby's answer, Jake turned his gaze from Elizabeth and studied the kid.

"Well, she's real polite."

"Yeah, and what else?"

"She hasn't said anything mean."

"I don't think she's the mean type," Jake said, "but I wouldn't be too sure of myself if I were you. I don't think she'll give up her niece easily."

"Aw, she'll come around. You're taking her off to see the sights tomorrow?"

"Yes, sir," Jake said, hiding a smile.

Bobby lowered his voice. "You don't have to go with us tonight. Amy said her aunt's tired and wants to go to bed instead of out on the town."

"Suit yourself," Jake said, knowing he wasn't going to sleep much tonight, not while knowing that Elizabeth was only a few hundred yards away. "You're not gonna get out of here without a chaperone, no matter how much you think the aunt likes you. Especially after that rolling-around-in-the-dirt stunt you pulled a while ago."

Bobby grinned. "It felt pretty darn good, too. That crazy Gus did me a favor."

Jake couldn't help feeling a little bit jealous.

4

"SOMETHING WRONG?"

Other than the fact that Jake had touched the small of her back and guided her through a crowd of beer-drinking Texans, Elizabeth couldn't think of a thing. Her brain had dissolved the moment his fingertips touched her spine. And it wasn't the first time.

"No," she said, straightening her shoulders and pretending her skin didn't burn under his touch. "I've just never seen so many...cowboys in one place before." Obviously Friday nights in Texas were taken seriously—there was serious dancing, serious drinking and serious flirting going on inside the Last Chance Bar, on the corner of Route 128 and East Main Road. Each Western man there looked as if he was doing all three at the same time. And the women—wearing tight jeans and tighter T-shirts—looked capable of keeping up with the men in every way.

Elizabeth hurried to follow Bobby as he led their group to a small table near the bar.

"Do you dance?" Jake asked.

"What?" She turned slightly, and Jake's head lowered, his lips almost grazing her ear.

"Dance," he said. "Do you?"

"Oh," she managed to reply, feeling like a teenager on her first date. She needed to get a grip. She needed a pair of boots and two feet that could actually move in unison. She needed to remember she was here to chaperone Amy. "Not really."

His eyebrows rose and he said something else, but the band's climactic ending to their song drowned out his words.

She thought she'd forgotten about the tiny cleft in his squared chin and the way his breath fanned her cheek with such intimacy. She wanted to turn toward him and remember what it had been like to kiss him the first time.

And the last.

"Not at all?"

She gestured toward the dance floor, where couples began the next dance. "Not—whatever it is they're doing."

"The two-step," he said, raising his voice to be heard over the music. "It's not that hard if you'd like to try it."

Elizabeth moved toward the table where Amy and her cowboy had settled and were busy talking to a waitress. "No, thank you."

Jake pulled out a seat for her before she could do

it for herself, so Elizabeth sat and smiled weakly across the table at her niece.

"Cool place," Amy said, tapping her fingers on the scarred table in time with the music. It was a song about broken hearts and cowboys, Elizabeth noted before she stopped listening. She leaned forward to hear Bobby's question.

"Drink?"

"Maybe a soda?"

He nodded, then left the table and headed toward the crowded bar. Jake went with him, which left Elizabeth alone to talk to her niece.

"We're not going to stay late," Elizabeth declared, repeating the sentence when Amy looked confused and leaned across the table.

"You're tired?"

"It's been a long day."

Her niece sighed. "Aunt B, you really ought to liven up. You're not exactly decrepit."

"No," Elizabeth said, looking around her at the jeans-clad crowd. "But I—we—don't belong here."

"I like it."

"For a vacation, maybe. But for the rest of your life?" Elizabeth shook her head. "You shouldn't make any hasty decisions."

"Decisions about what?" Jake asked, putting a drink in front of her.

"Nothing," she said, watching Amy's attention being claimed by Bobby, who set bottles of beer on the table before tugging Amy to the dance floor. The band had switched to a waltz.

"It's not easy taking care of them, is it?"

Surprised, Elizabeth turned to face Jake. "Is that what you've done with Bobby?"

"Yeah. Since he was a kid."

She didn't want to have a personal conversation with him. She didn't want to like him or to think they had things in common. And she didn't want him to ask again about Chicago, so Elizabeth took a sip of her drink. "What is this?"

"Whiskey and soda."

"I didn't—never mind," Elizabeth replied, realizing that Bobby hadn't heard her correctly. The drink didn't taste too terrible, and a few drops of whiskey might be exactly what she needed to numb her senses.

Jake sat down, and moved his chair closer to hers. His knee bumped her leg, and Elizabeth quickly took another sip of her drink.

"We can dance if you want."

She didn't look at him and kept her attention focused on the couples on the dance floor. Amy twirled past, laughing at her handsome young man. Amy had always been coordinated and brave. "I'd rather watch."

"It's easy to learn." He put down his beer and scraped his chair back. Standing up, he held out his hand to her.

It shouldn't have been irresistible, Elizabeth told herself later. She shouldn't have automatically reached up and placed her hand in Jake's. Later on, tossing between white sheets in the quiet bedroom, she would wonder why she had gone like a magnet to him and let him weave her through the crowd and take her in his arms. She would tell herself that he didn't have a clue that she was the same woman who fell into his arms last February, who tiptoed out of his hotel room and thought she'd never ever have to divulge what she'd done. She would close the curtains against the Texas moon and promise herself to be gone within forty-eight hours, no matter what Amy said or did.

But for now, she was in his arms. He didn't smile. Instead he counted the beats out loud for her to follow as he held her waist and her hand and guided her through the steps.

They danced two fast songs without stopping for breath, with Jake holding her several inches away from his body so she could look at her feet and count the beats along with him. She only stumbled twice. Then an enthusiastic Texan knocked her against Jake's hard chest, and she suddenly forgot how to count to two.

"WHAT ARE YOU going to do with her?"

Jake ignored the question and nodded toward the

six horses prancing in the corral. "What are you going to do with *them?*"

Bobby leaned against the fence and watched Jake sip his steaming mug of coffee. "I'll get the job done," Bobby promised. "Amy wants to see what I do. You're not going to go back on the deal, are you? I mean, you're taking the auntie off to see quilts or stuff like that, right?"

Jake rested his arms on the top railing of the fence and tried to hide his smile. He looked at the horses instead of the kid. "Antique shops," he said. "We're heading south to Marysville."

"Marysville?" Bobby's voice brightened. "That's two hours from here."

"Yeah." Jake had gotten out the Texas guidebook he'd bought last week and altered his plans for the ancient auntie. There were plenty of stores closer to the ranch, but Jake wasn't interested in making this a short day. Not for what he intended, which was to keep Elizabeth with him until dark. "We might not be back for dinner," he said, turning toward Bobby. "But I'm sure you don't mind."

"Heck, no," the kid said, grinning like he'd just won a round of poker. "Amy and I can figure out something to do."

"Not with Mrs. Martin watching you, you won't."

The kid shrugged. "I can figure something out."

"Keep your hands off the girl until you know if

you're getting married." Jake held Bobby's gaze. "Or the only place I'm going today is to town to order more feed."

"Geez, Jake," Bobby groaned. "This isn't fair."

"So?" Jake took another sip of coffee and wondered what he would do if the boy didn't agree. He'd be hard pressed to give up his day with Elizabeth, but he damn well wasn't going to leave here with Bobby thinking he could do whatever he wanted with his guest. If Elizabeth thought her niece and Bobby were having sex in the barn—and anywhere else they damn well pleased—he'd never get her to go off with him again. "You can save the fireworks for your wedding night."

"I'd better get married pretty damn soon," Bobby grumbled, shoving his hands in his pockets and turning toward the house. "Come on, Gus," he said, as the dog galloped around the corner of the feed shed.

"You'll survive," Jake said, thinking of his own sleepless night knowing Elizabeth was within driving distance.

"I didn't think you'd be like this, Jake."

He wasn't sure why he was acting this way, either, except he wanted Bobby married and settled as soon as possible. And he wanted Elizabeth back in his bed. Also as soon as possible. "The ladies are our guests. *Your* guests," Jake amended. "There's no way the aunt is going to leave you alone with Amy if she thinks you're up to no good."

"Well, I want the aunt to like me."

"Yesterday's roll in the dirt wasn't exactly getting off to the right start." He clapped the boy on the shoulder and started off toward the ranch house. "Let's go see if the women are up yet." He looked at his watch. "I wouldn't mind being on the road by nine. And you promised to do my work, too, today, so I could haul Aunt B around, remember?"

"Yeah."

"There's bills to pay," Jake reminded him as they approached the back door. "And you'll need to balance the accounts and—"

"Whoa," Bobby yelped. He hesitated before the door and didn't let Gus inside. "You're piling it on, aren't you?"

Jake shrugged and tried not to laugh. "Just a typical Saturday, kid. You're usually so hung over from Friday night that you sleep until afternoon on Saturday. It's good to see you up so early."

Bobby swore under his breath, but grinned the second the door opened and Amy was on the other side smiling at him.

"I thought I heard you," she said, looking extremely pretty in faded jeans and a pink tank top. Jake felt sorry for Bobby until he reminded himself of the havoc the young man had caused since he was twelve and discovered girls.

"Yeah," Bobby said, sounding a little breathless. "We were talking about the horses. I've got a busy day ahead of me."

Amy looked enchanted. "Can I go with you?"

"You can watch," he offered, looking over at Elizabeth. "Good mornin'."

"Good morning." Elizabeth sat at the kitchen table, a coffee cup in front of her. She looked gorgeous, Jake noted. Her gold-streaked hair was tied off her face, exposing a slender neck.

Mrs. Martin turned away from the stove and motioned with a spatula. "Sit down, boys, and I'll cook up some eggs for you."

"I ate at home, but thanks," Jake told her, going to the counter. "I appreciate the coffee, though."

"I'll show Amy the horses while you two plan your day," Bobby said, taking Amy by the hand as he lead her outside.

Jake refilled his cup and started to sit down at the table across from Elizabeth. This wasn't going to be easy, but he didn't intend to let her get her way and avoid him. She'd danced with him last night, even though she'd said she didn't dance. And he'd been careful to keep her inches away from him, as if she really were some eighty-year-old auntie come to Texas to visit.

"Watch out," Elizabeth said, leaning toward the floor.

"What?" He spilled a few drops of coffee on his hand and swore softly.

"I'll have none of that language around here," Mrs. Martin declared. "And don't put your chair on that dog."

"He's in his bed on the floor," Elizabeth said, straightening.

Jake looked down as he moved the chair. The ball of fur was curled up in a bed. Jake couldn't tell if the thing was dead or alive, but he decided he'd better not insult her dog again. "Sorry."

"You've planned the day?" Elizabeth asked, those green eyes gazing at him with a guarded expression. "I'm sorry I don't know much about horses."

"You don't have to. I'm leaving that job to Bobby."

"And it's about time, too," Mrs. Martin said, scrubbing the frying pan. Soap splattered on the counter beside her, but she didn't notice. "That boy needs to spend more time working and less time playing, if you ask me."

"He'll put in a full day's work today," Jake said. "I talked to Marty and he's going to do errands in town, so if there's anything you need, give him a list." He hoped a grocery list would distract her from saying anything more about Bobby that would give Elizabeth the wrong idea. "Ms. Comstock and I are heading to Marysville."

"Marysville? Whatever for?" the housekeeper asked.

"Yes," said Elizabeth, looking at him as if he was up to no good, which he was. "What's in Marysville?"

"Antique stores," he replied. "Lots of them. Amy Lou told Bobby you like shopping for old things."

"I do, but—"

"Oh, you'll like it there," Mrs. Martin—bless her cranky heart—declared. "Just about everyone does, though I don't know why people spend good money on that old stuff. Some of those things they try to sell you have *rust* on them."

"Rust?" Jake said indignantly.

"It's very popular right now," Elizabeth explained in a soft voice.

"So, you *do* like shopping for this kind of stuff?" Jake asked.

"Well, yes, but—"

"We can leave whenever you're ready," he said, cutting off any objections he figured she'd make.

"But Amy—"

"Can take care of your, uh, Pook," he said, looking down at the sleeping animal. "He could probably use the exercise."

Elizabeth shook her head. "He's not really an outside kind of dog."

Jake looked hopefully at the temporary housekeeper. "I'll keep my eye on your niece," Mrs. Martin promised, swiping the counter with a damp sponge. "But I'm not baby-sitting that animal and I'm not cleaning up after him, either."

"I think I should stay here," Elizabeth said. "Amy and I can watch Bobby and the horses and you can do whatever it is that ranch foremen do."

The only thing he wanted to do at the moment couldn't be accomplished without shocking Mrs. Martin, so Jake settled for drinking coffee.

"I don't want to take you away from your work," Elizabeth continued.

"Jake works all the time," Mrs. Martin declared, her hands on her hips. "It's about time that Bobby did his share. Won't hurt him a bit to settle down and take up the reins around here. Then maybe my Marty will do the same thing and I can get some grandchildren instead of worrying 'bout those boys gallivanting all over the county drinking beer and doing Lord knows what with Lord knows who." With that said, she retreated to the sink and started the dishwasher.

"So," Jake said, turning to the beautiful woman with the problem dog and the pretty niece and asked the question he knew no woman could refuse. "Do you want to go shopping?"

Elizabeth frowned at him, as if she wondered if he was trying to trick her, which he was, of course. "We won't be gone too long?"

The sound of the dishwasher kept Mrs. Martin from hearing his answer. "No."

"All right, then."

"Can you be ready in twenty minutes?" Jake asked Elizabeth.

She nodded, so Jake took off. He paid Shorty twenty bucks to baby-sit the dog. He promised Marty an extra day off if he promised to make sure that Bobby was never alone with his lady love. He found an old Stetson for Amy to wear and steered clear of Mrs. Martin, who was vacuuming with a vengeance and muttering to herself.

And he opened the passenger door of Bobby's Cadillac for Elizabeth and waited for her to seat herself inside. He couldn't believe his luck.

It was all going according to plan.

SHE SHOULD HAVE been stronger. But when faced with a choice between watching Amy gaze adoringly at her cowboy for the rest of the morning, sitting in her room with Pookie to avoid doing anything to upset Mrs. Martin and going to a nearby town to shop for antiques, Elizabeth made a selfish decision.

She was sure she could handle Jake. Besides, avoiding him would only make him think that she had something to be embarrassed about. That she was the woman he thought she was. But last night he appeared to have accepted her denial, had acted like a perfect gentleman, had driven them all back to the ranch and said good-night almost absentmindedly, as if he'd forgotten they existed at all.

He was doing his duty, entertaining the aunt. That's all it was.

"You put a lot of thought into this," she said, once they were on the main road.

"What do you mean?"

"Finding out what I liked to do. Locating antique shops."

"I lost at poker." Jake smiled at her before turning his attention back to the road ahead. Elizabeth realized exactly how handsome he was. "So I got you."

The statement seemed funny to her. "You got Amy's Aunt B?"

"Yes, ma'am. I'm to chaperone the elderly auntie and make sure she has a good time."

"I'm really sorry," she managed to say, but she couldn't help laughing. She even forgot for a moment that she was embarrassed about February. And nervous to be alone with him. "You must have had terrible cards."

"Worst hands of my life," he said. "I lost twenty-one dollars, too."

"I should buy you lunch."

He glanced toward her again, but this time his expression was serious. "You also owe me breakfast, Beth."

She was too surprised to pretend she didn't know

what he was talking about. Elizabeth stared at the expanse of land that stretched toward the horizon. There was nothing to see except distant fences and an occasional outbuilding.

"Could we at least get this out in the open?" Jake asked. "I'm not much for games."

"Neither am I."

"No?" He glanced in the rearview mirror, then slowed the car to park on the side of the road. There wasn't another car in sight as he switched off the engine and turned to face her. "You want to get this over with?"

More than anything, she thought, unless she could continue to pretend it never happened. "This is very embarrassing."

"Why?" He frowned.

"I never thought I'd see you again," she said, facing him.

"But you have. So?"

"So...I don't know what to say." She knew her face was hot, despite the air-conditioned coolness inside the car. "I don't expect you to believe me, but I've never done anything like that before in my life."

"I don't make a habit of making love with strangers either," he said, a half-smile creasing his tanned face. "But you can't expect me to act like it didn't happen."

"I really wish you would."

He shook his head. "No way, lady. That was one hell of a snowstorm. And one hell of a night."

"WE'RE ALONE," Bobby said, grinning at Amy Lou.

He really was the cutest thing, she thought once again. And when he took her hand and pulled her closer, she didn't resist. Not one bit.

"I hope Aunt B has a good time," she said, feeling the tiniest bit guilty about sending her aunt off with that quiet Jake Johnson. "I don't think she likes Jake very much."

Bobby tugged her toward the hay barn. "Everybody likes Jake, once they get to know him."

"Where are we going?"

"The barn."

"Why?" She hurried to match his long strides. "What about training the horses?"

"They can wait," he said, grinning at her. "I can't."

Amy giggled, thinking of various wonderful things that could be done in the privacy of a hayloft. "Is that why you're in such a hurry?"

He stopped and tugged her against him.

He was hard in all the right places, she noted, feeling a thrill at the thought of being alone with him. They'd never actually done it, though they'd come close a few times at her roommate's home.

"Honey," he groaned, tickling her earlobe with his lips. "If Mrs. Martin hadn't stopped talking to

you about vacuum cleaners, I would have hurt myself."

"Hey!"

Amy peered around Bobby's shoulder to see
Marty coming toward them. "Hi," she said, as
Bobby swore under his breath and draped his arm
around her shoulder.

"What?" Bobby asked in an irritated tone.

"Jake said I'm supposed to help you with the
horses today." He tipped his hat to Amy. "Hi,
there."

"Later." Bobby tried to insist.

"Hi," Amy replied, wishing Bobby didn't sound
so rude. They were going to have hours alone together, so one little conversation couldn't hurt.

"Jake said," Marty insisted. "And there'll be hell
to pay if I don't do what he said. I'm not gonna
spend my day off mucking out stalls, that's for
sure."

"Jeez," Bobby sighed. "Can't you give a guy a
break?"

"Nope." Marty winked at Amy. "I hope you
don't mind, Amy Lou, but we've got work to do."

"I don't mind," she replied, giving Bobby a smile.
"You said you were going to show me how you
train horses, remember? And maybe there'd be time
to go for a ride?"

"A ride?" Marty grinned. "The twins wanted to

come out this afternoon, so we could all go somewhere together."

"I'm not a very good rider," Amy admitted. "But I'd like to see more of the ranch."

"Don't worry, honey," Bobby said, giving Marty a dirty look. "I'll give you the grand tour. Marty, why don't you start with the pinto pony and I'll catch up with you in a while?"

Amy blushed to think that Marty would know why they were going to the barn and what they might be doing in there. "No, Bobby. I'm not going to keep you from your work." She ducked out from under his arm and took his hand. "Show me what a cowboy does."

He tugged her against him and lowered his voice. "Honey, I'll be glad to do that if you'll go with me to the barn."

Amy laughed, tempted once again, but Marty interrupted them. "Oh, yeah," he said. "Shorty wanted me to tell you that he can't find your dog."

"What?" she asked.

"Huh?" Bobby shrugged. "Gus is always around here somewhere."

"Not Gus," Marty said. "The little guy. What's his name?"

"Pookie?" Amy squeaked. "He's lost?"

"Well," the cowboy drawled. "Just for a while."

"Oh, my God," Amy said, looking around the

vast area of ranch buildings and fences. Everything looked dangerous, considering Pookie's size and trusting nature. "Aunt B's going to have a fit! Once I get married, he's the only thing she'll have left."

5

"IT'S GOING TO BE *one hell of a night*," he'd said, setting his duffel bag beside her suitcase as he joined her at the end of a line of people at the airline's check in counter. She'd turned to see a tall man dressed in jeans and a leather jacket standing behind her. Snowflakes dotted his dark Stetson and the shoulders of the barn jacket. He looked completely out of place in an airport full of resigned businesspeople and frantic families.

She'd looked at her watch. "It's only two o'clock."

"Yeah," he'd said, looking unconcerned as he gave her a quick grin. "And I figure we're going to be here all night."

"I hope you're wrong," she'd replied, then turned to face the checkout counter. The clerks continued to look frazzled and defeated, but then this was Chicago in February and no one should have been surprised when a monster of a snowstorm threatened to change their traveling plans.

She felt a tap on her shoulder and turned around. She hoped this man wasn't going to be a pest.

"Excuse me," he said. "Can I leave this bag with you? I'm going to make a phone call."

She looked past him and saw that they were no longer at the end of the line. "All right," Elizabeth had said, wondering at the same time if she was breaking some unwritten rule of airport etiquette or merely being polite to a stranger. He'd smiled, and she felt her heart stop for a second. She'd wondered later if it was a reaction to the Stetson. She didn't see many of those in Rhode Island.

"Thanks. I'll be back real soon."

And of course he wasn't, since the lines at the phones were as long as the lines at the airline counters. But this line wasn't moving, either, and Elizabeth didn't have to nudge his duffel bag more than six feet before the cowboy—because that's all she could think of to call him—returned looking pleased with himself.

"There," he said, joining her in line as if they were a couple traveling together. "Thanks."

"You're welcome." She smiled at him, despite her intention to remain aloof. Befriending strangers in airports was not something she did. She'd never been one of those people who found it easy to talk to people she didn't know well.

"I had to see if I could get my room back," he explained. His voice had a slight Western drawl Elizabeth found comforting. After all, everyone knew that Westerners were friendly and hospitable. Or so she told herself.

"Oh." It was all she could think of to reply. He had blue eyes that looked straight at her. A friendly, direct gaze, not at all intimidating, she thought.

"Yep. I had to do some fast talking, they said I could

have it back." He glanced behind him, where they both saw that at least fifty people had joined the line. "I have a feeling we're not going anywhere tonight."

The thought was exactly what she didn't want to face. She peered around the large man in front of her and checked the departing-flights board on the wall. Her flight to Providence, scheduled to depart an hour ago, was still listed as delayed.

"I hope you're wrong," she said. "I have to be at work in the morning."

"So you don't live here," the cowboy said.

"No." She glanced at the board again, just to reassure herself that her flight was still listed. "I've been here since ten."

"Why?"

"I thought I'd better get here early, since it was snowing." She grimaced. "I should have known everything would be delayed."

The line moved forward a couple of feet and the cowboy bent down and moved her suitcase forward for her. He wore polished brown cowboy boots with pointed toes and decorated leather.

"Thank you," she offered. They'd stood for a few moments in silence, with Elizabeth wishing she'd eaten more for breakfast than a bagel and coffee. She glanced at her watch again, and the line inched forward another foot. Elizabeth wanted to go home, wanted to sink into her warm bed and watch Masterpiece Theatre on television tonight. She'd hoped to be home by nine, but even she had *to admit that the odds of being stuck in O'Hare Airport were increasing. Outside there was nothing to see except swirling snow and the gray outlines of planes and trucks. Anything that moved was doing it slowly. She wondered if she should try to get her hotel room back, or even if she would be able to find a taxi to return her downtown.*

She wondered if she'd be spending all day and maybe all night in the airport.

She'd always been good at worrying.

JAKE STARTED the car. He wasn't going to push his luck by breaking the silence between them. Jake figured Elizabeth was going to come around eventually, especially now that he'd gotten her to admit she knew exactly who he was and where they'd met. He drove through Beauville and pointed out the local landmarks.

"Steak Barn," he said, pointing to a two-story restaurant on the corner of Main and Cotton. "Best steak in the county. Next to it is J.C. Penney's, if you want to do any shopping." He drove slowly down the next block. "Movie theater, gift shop, real estate, insurance." Then, "The library. Round the corner is a grocery store."

She obligingly looked out the window. "It looks exactly like I thought a small town in Texas would look."

"And that is?" he prompted.

"Very Western." She turned toward him and

smiled. "The buildings look like they're from a cowboy movie."

"Yeah, some of them do. Old Man Jackson has tried to preserve some of the old buildings." Another block and they were out of town. "Over there was the Good Night Drive-In."

"Was?"

"It's been closed for years. I guess that's something else that's considered old-fashioned."

"I suppose. I don't think I've ever been to one."

"You missed out," he told her.

"How far away is Marysville?"

"A little over an hour."

She stared at him, then looked out the window again. There wasn't much to see, he figured. Just fences and dusty roads, windmills and an occasional house. She'd soon tire of the scenery.

And then she'd have to talk to him again.

SHE'D BEEN incredibly beautiful, despite the worried expression as she studied the departure board on the wall above the ticket agents' desk. He'd wondered if a husband or boyfriend would join her in line, claim her as his. But no, his luck had held, and the beautiful woman with the long chestnut hair and jade green eyes was alone. And he'd spoken to her and made her smile.

That smile had just about knocked him on his derriere.

He'd sensed trouble before it happened, heard the tense conversation escalate as three men built like wrestlers lost their temper with the ticket agent. They swore, a litany of curses not fit for women and children to hear, and one of them pounded the counter while the other attempted to climb over it. His backpack flew toward the woman's feet.

"Watch out," Jake said as he stepped in front of her, protecting her from what was sure to be a fight. They were next in line, too close to trouble. He leaned forward and grabbed one young man by the collar of his shirt, lifting him off the floor an inch and holding him tight. "Tell your friends to quit this now," he demanded, tightening his grip on the kid's shirt.

"Mark, Dave," he gurgled. "Cool it."

Two airport security officers appeared just as Mark or Dave threw a wild punch at the male ticket agent, a skinny young man who looked as if he hadn't slept in a week. They managed to get all three men to calm down, rounded up their luggage, then took them away.

"You okay?" he asked, joining the woman back in line.

"Fine, thank you." She'd seemed shy, surprising in a woman so beautiful. "That was nice of you, but—"

"But?"

"Dangerous," she finished.

He shrugged. "They shouldn't have lost their tempers. You're next."

"What?"

He'd nodded toward the counter. "To check in."

"Oh." She'd smiled again, then picked up her luggage and moved to the counter. She looked over her shoulder at him as he waited in line.

The board changed; all flights were canceled. It was going to be a long day in O'Hare, Jake realized. But maybe, just maybe, the woman would smile at him again. For some reason he felt like they were in this mess together.

ANTIQUES were a mistake. He realized it too late, after Elizabeth disappeared into a building crowded with aisle after aisle of old stuff. He'd just given her the perfect way to avoid him.

Jake tried to keep up without knocking anything over. He got hung up when he tripped on a box of tools that were sticking out into the aisle, but caught up with her when she paused in front of a set of china, the kind of stuff that looked like it would break if you tried to cut a piece of beef on it. He watched as she gently picked up a teacup and turned it upside down to examine it closer.

He managed to stand beside her but stayed back from the table. "What are you looking for?"

"The manufacturer," she said, holding the cup toward him. "See?"

"Limoges," he read. "Is that important?"

"It can be." She set the little pink and white cup on the table filled with all sorts of china. "If that's what you like."

"Do you?"

"Sometimes. It depends on the colors." She moved to a display of dish towels, fingering each one. He wondered if she was trying to avoid him, since no one could be that interested in old towels, could they?

"So Amy was right," he said, stepping over a copper bowl filled with dried flowers. "You do like old stuff."

"I love it," she murmured, moving on to a shelf filled with glassware. Jake watched as she checked the prices on some pink colored sets of goblets, then ran the tip of her finger around the rims in a delicate motion.

"You never know what you're going to find," she said.

"Yeah," he said, hoping he sounded like he knew what she was talking about. He figured there wasn't much point to shopping unless you knew what you wanted to buy in the first place.

Elizabeth looked like she was having fun, had maybe even forgotten she was supposed to be chaperoning her lively little niece.

"What were you doing in Chicago, by the way? You never told me."

She didn't take her eyes off the display of crystal. "Chicago didn't happen."

"Our night in Chicago didn't happen, the wedding isn't going to happen. Has anyone ever told you you're not very realistic?"

"I have a firm grip on reality."

He didn't look convinced.

She plucked a ruby goblet from a tray filled with

glasses of various shapes and colors and looked at the price. "Now here's a bargain." She checked the rim and the base for chips, then turned to Jake. "It's only two dollars."

"But there's only one of them."

"That's all I need," she said, turning away from him to explore another shelf of glassware.

"I wanted to get around to that." Jake hurried to keep up with her, but she'd paused in front of a rack of patchwork quilts.

"Around to what?" She bent and looked for a price tag, then drew in her breath.

"If I had any competition."

"Would you hold this for a second?" She gave him the ruby glass and then began to unfold a quilt that looked as if it had spent the last twenty years in a barn.

"That's the worst-looking log cabin quilt I've ever seen," he declared as Elizabeth held it up.

"How do you know what kind it is?"

He shrugged. "My mother had a few of them."

"Lucky you."

"I have a couple in my bedroom," he said. "I can show them to you." He grinned as she glanced in his direction.

"Thanks, but no thanks," she said.

Jake watched as she folded the brown quilt and examined two others. "You like quilts," he said.

"Yes."

"I bought tickets to a quilt show." He thought that should get him some points.

"For Amy's old-lady aunt." She gave the quilts one last yearning look before moving on to a display of silver.

"Yeah."

"When?"

"Sunday."

She didn't look at him. "We'll be leaving that day."

"Unless you're staying for a wedding."

Elizabeth picked up a calico doll and then set it gently back on its chair. "There won't be a wedding."

"You could be wrong."

Her chin lifted. "So could you."

"Want to bet?" He had her complete attention, which pleased him no end.

"No."

"If you win and there's no wedding, I'll pick up the tab on one of these quilts. You pick which one."

"And if there is a wedding? What do you want?"

"What you've told me I can't have."

She blushed, then looked around the empty store to make sure no one was listening. "I'm not betting—well, you know what I'm not betting," she whispered.

"I want a date," he said, pretending he didn't

know what she was talking about. "At the drive-in."

"It's closed."

"We can pretend." He knew if he got her to himself in a car, at night, all alone, well, then it would just about be the perfect evening.

"Aren't you a little old for parking in cars?"

"Maybe," he said, trying not to laugh. "Maybe not. There's only one way to find out."

"There won't be a wedding," she repeated, plucking the goblet out of his hand without touching him. "And I think we'd better get back to the ranch now."

"But it's lunchtime."

"I'm not hungry."

"Mrs. Martin is chaperoning the kids," he reminded her. "And I paid Marty—you remember Marty?"

"The one who inherited the twins."

"Right." He wanted to bend down and kiss her on those peachy pink lips of hers. Elizabeth Comstock was entirely too self-assured. "I paid him extra to keep Amy and Bobby out of the hayloft."

"You have my heartfelt gratitude."

"You're very welcome," he said, tipping his hat to make her smile. "And didn't you say you owed me lunch?"

"I did," she answered, ignoring another display of old linens. "In that case I think I'll have a double bacon cheeseburger with fries. And a chocolate shake."

"You saw the hamburger stand across the street, I guess?"

"I can't resist junk food," she admitted, heading toward the counter where a bored clerk read a magazine and swatted flies.

"I know," he called after her. "That's how I found you again, remember?"

SHE DIDN'T SEE HIM *again until after she'd learned the flights were canceled and it was likely that no planes would be flying for the rest of the afternoon. According to the weather reports, the clerk explained, the storm was only going to worsen and the snow wasn't expected to stop until after midnight.*

Elizabeth waited in line for twenty minutes before getting a telephone, then called the hotel only to learn that they were full. Which meant it was going to be a very long day. Luckily she had a book in her handbag, plenty of cash, and there were restaurants in the main section of the concourse. She ended up in line at the hamburger stand, only to realize that the cowboy was in line at another food stand next to her. It would have been easy to miss him in the crowd, except she felt someone looking at her and glanced over to see him wink.

The cowboy seemed like more of an old friend than a threatening stranger this time, so she'd smiled back. Doing so seemed harmless enough, especially in an airport food court surrounded by people. After she'd placed her order and had a tray piled high with lunch, she saw him again.

He was waiting for her. He'd snagged a table and two chairs, one of which was obviously for her. So Elizabeth ate lunch with the most handsome man she'd ever seen in her twenty-nine years.

"Thank you again for helping out with those men back there," she said.

"I couldn't let a lovely lady like yourself get hit by a backpack, could I?"

She ignored the compliment. And the flirtation. "Do you do that kind of thing often?"

"When it's necessary," he said, tearing the wrapper off a taco. "I'm a Texan, born and bred. We don't believe in backing down from a fight."

"I can believe it." She held out her hand. "I'm...Beth."

He took it, sending a jolt of awareness through her. "Jake."

"Nice to meet you," she said, knowing she sounded ridiculous as they smiled at each other. There was something about all that testosterone that was oddly appealing, Elizabeth realized. And something about being stranded in a snowstorm that made her want to sit in the food court with the cowboy for the next few hours. He was safe...or else she felt safe when she was with him.

And she was so darn tired of being lonely. She couldn't remember what they talked about over lunch, but he told her Texas stories and she listened and laughed. She bought them large cups of coffee from a concession. They shared his newspaper; she left her luggage with him while she went to the ladies' rest room.

The storm worsened. People began to stake out chairs and benches on which to nap. The restaurants began to run out of food, since trucks hadn't been able to make deliveries. More flights were canceled, more unintelligible announcements made on the loudspeakers.

"Look," he said, leaning toward her so she could hear him. A group of teenagers had landed at the table next to them, CD player blasting the latest pop hit. "This is crazy. I've got a hotel room," he said. "You're welcome to share it."

"I can't."

"It's right here, next to the airport," he said. "You'd be more comfortable in the hotel, I think. I can sleep in the lobby."

"I can't take your room."

"You're not taking it, I'm giving it to you. Nobody's going to get out of here until tomorrow." He motioned around him at the crowds of people. "Tell me you don't want to spend the night here."

"I don't, but—"

"Then come on," he said, picking up both their bags. "You can buy me a drink after we get rid of these bags."

"You could have been in your hotel hours ago."

"Yeah," he said, looking at her with those gorgeous blue eyes of his. "But this is a hell of a lot more fun."

"I FIGURED we were going to be alone all day," Bobby grumbled, following Amy toward the ranch house. Gus, who was trying desperately to sniff Pookie, trailed behind them.

"Me, too," Amy said, cradling her little dog in her arms. She'd wondered what it would be like to make love to Bobby more times than she wanted to admit. And kissing in the hay barn had sounded like a great beginning to a romantic Western weekend.

"Shorty should have looked harder before telling Marty the darn dog was lost." He stopped in front of the corral that held six prancing mares.

"I should have told him that Pookie likes to get under the covers." Amy sighed, thinking of getting under the covers with Bobby. She'd never been promiscuous, but Bobby Calhoun's wicked kisses could tempt a nun.

Bobby frowned at the dog. "You want to take the little guy back to the house?"

"Not yet. I don't think Mrs. Martin likes dogs."

"Not in her kitchen," he agreed, leaning on the fence. He smiled at her. "You want to watch me act like a cowboy?"

"Sure." She swore her heart beat faster.

"Stay here, honey, and I'll show you what we do around here." He gave her a quick kiss before climbing over the fence. She watched as he collected leather and rope paraphernalia hanging from a nearby post and then prepared herself to be fascinated by Bobby's skill with horses.

Marty sauntered up to join her. "The boss putting on a show?"

"I hope so."

"You gonna marry him?"

Amy shook her head. "That's none of your business," she said, just like she hadn't thought about marrying Bobby about every five minutes.

"Marty!" Bobby waved at him. "Come get this bay out of here!"

"Coming!" But Marty didn't move. "Truth is, ma'am, that there's some betting going on about this wedding and I could sure use the extra money." He winked at her.

"Do cowboys bet on everything?"

"Pretty much." He took off his hat, scratched his head, then replaced the hat, the brim lower across his brow. "I think folks are bettin' on which twin I'll end up with. It's nothin' to take offense at."

"Okay." She turned to the corral and her almost-fiancé. Aunt B liked him, despite what she said about how different their lives were. Who couldn't love Bobby?

"Ma'am?"

"Hmm?" She thought Bobby looked wonderful as he led the snorting horse her way. It looked wild, but Bobby didn't seem to be afraid at all.

"The bet?"

"You'll be the first to know," Amy assured him. Tonight, she promised herself. Tonight she and Bobby would be alone together, no matter what Aunt B said or did about it.

Tonight there was going to be a full moon, a moon made for romance. Aunt B was just going to have to understand.

6

"A MIDNIGHT RIDE? Neither one of us has ever been on a horse before," Elizabeth said. "Doing it for the first time in the dark sounds suicidal."

"Not exactly at midnight, just when it gets dark. There's a full moon," her niece explained. "It will be romantic."

Romantic was the last thing she wanted to be, especially when she was around Jake. Elizabeth settled Pookie in his bed beside hers and wished she was a million miles away. Or at least two thousand miles, in her safe little summerhouse.

"And you haven't spent much time with Bobby," her niece continued, while fixing her hair in front of the mirror. "You want to get to know him better, don't you?"

"I want to go home," she said, petting the little dog. *Before I make another mistake. Before I embarrass myself again. Before you do something you might regret for the rest of your life.* "And I want to take you with me."

Amy turned to gaze at her with horror. "Not yet, Aunt B, please!"

Elizabeth closed her eyes and sank back against the pillows. She'd spent most of her day acting as if Jake was a perfectly ordinary man showing her the antique stores in his part of Texas. She'd kept her shoulders straight and her smile pleasant and she'd tried very hard not to talk about Chicago and what they'd done there together.

"Are you sick?" Amy asked.

"No." Elizabeth opened her eyes to see Amy's face a foot away. "Why on earth do you want to get married, honey? You're only twenty-one."

"I'm ready. And I'm in love."

"Being in love has nothing to do with it. You just *think* you're in love."

Amy put her hands over her ears and grinned. "What, Aunt B? I can't hear you."

"I should give up," Elizabeth told Pookie, who looked very sleepy. "I should leave her here and you and I should go back to New England."

"Not until after you learn how to ride," Amy said, taking her hand. "Come on. Mrs. Martin cooked something that smells wonderful, and Bobby will be waiting for us."

And Jake, too, no doubt. She didn't know whether to run downstairs or hide under the covers. Elizabeth took a deep breath and heaved herself off the bed. What was she so anxious about? They'd talked about Chicago, and there was nothing else to say. Surely the worst was over.

She was sure of it hours later, after having a roast beef dinner with Bobby. Jake was nowhere to be seen, thank goodness. She told herself she was relieved and not disappointed. Bobby was charming, entertaining them with stories of life on the ranch. Of course Amy hung on his every word, and Elizabeth knew her niece pictured herself riding—and possibly roping—with the best of them here on the range.

Elizabeth had her doubts about straddling a horse and trotting off into the moonlight, but Amy wouldn't hear her refusals. And Elizabeth couldn't let her niece go off into the dark with a young man whose testosterone levels were higher than his IQ. It was almost dark when they changed into jeans and put on the long-sleeved shirts Bobby lent them.

"It'll be fun," Amy insisted, hauling Elizabeth across the yard toward the biggest barn. "Jake's going to make sure that you're safe."

"He is?" She actually felt the heels of her borrowed boots dig into the dirt.

"Sure. Don't you like him?"

"Whether I like him or not doesn't have anything to do with anything." Elizabeth peered through the dusk and thought she saw Jake's large form in the barn doorway. Oh, no. Didn't he have anything else to do besides act as a tour guide? And tomorrow he had tickets to a quilt show, something a ninety-year-old woman would enjoy.

And she herself would love. A Texas quilt might be a perfect souvenir of this trip, if she decided she wanted to remember it. Elizabeth sighed. "I've never been comfortable around horses."

"Me, either," Amy admitted, hauling her aunt closer to the barn where two men led horses out the door and toward the women. "But it's time to be brave."

"Brave?" Jake stopped a horse in front of Elizabeth. "Is Ms. Comstock afraid of horses?"

She eyed the brown beast with the white patch on its forehead. Its mane was a shade lighter than the rest of him, and he surveyed her with calm brown eyes. "Yes."

"You've never ridden?" Jake asked.

"No." She ignored Jake's smile and eyed the horse. "What's his name?"

"Rocket."

"Uh-oh." She was going to die. She just knew it. Jake took her wrist gently between his fingers and placed her right hand on the horse's nose.

"Say hello," he ordered, keeping his hand on hers as she touched the velvet area of Rocket's head. She didn't know if the goose bumps on her arm came from touching the horse or being touched by the cowboy.

"He doesn't bite?"

Jake bent down to her, keeping his voice low. "None of us do."

There was a brief instant where she thought he was going to kiss her. But then his jaw set and he lifted his head and motioned to the saddle. "Get on."

"How?"

"Put your left foot in the stirrup and swing your right leg over. Always mount from the left and you'll stay out of trouble."

She glanced at her niece, who was being lifted into the saddle by her adoring cowboy. Leave it to Amy to make this look easy when it wasn't. "Okay."

Jake stepped back to give Elizabeth room. "Grab the saddle horn—that thing on top of the saddle—if you need to."

She needed more than a saddle horn when the horse sidestepped to the right and wouldn't let her climb on. "Rocket doesn't like this," she announced, trying to sound casual as she attempted to get her foot in the stirrup again.

"Whoa," Jake said, holding the horse's head. "Try again."

She did, only this time the horse stomped his foot as if he was impatient with visitors, and Elizabeth hesitated, one foot in the stirrup. "I hope this is the hardest part of the night."

"Not anymore," Jake said, walking behind her. "Here we go," he said, giving her derriere a push and vaulting her into the saddle.

Elizabeth grabbed the saddle horn and balanced herself. Surely she was tingling from fear and not lust. "Thank you."

"Yeah," he muttered, fiddling with the stirrup. "Get your leg out of the way for a second." He adjusted leather straps and then took her ankle into his large hand and guided her foot into the stirrup. Then he did the same on the other side, the efficient touch of his hands strangely intimate, though Elizabeth could tell he could do this chore in his sleep.

"You're all set," he said. "Pick up the reins and don't go anywhere till I get back."

"You're leaving me alone with the horse?"

"Yes, ma'am. For about ten seconds. Can you manage?"

She nodded, afraid that anything she said would be interpreted as giddap by Rocket, who would then live up to his name and proceed to gallop across Texas. She carefully turned her head to watch Amy being kissed while on horseback, which meant her niece was feeling a lot more comfortable five feet up in the air than her aunt was.

"We're all set," Jake said, leading a very large black horse up to hers. He swung easily into the saddle and gathered up the reins. Elizabeth hurried to imitate the way he held the leather reins and guided his horse.

"Left rein on the neck means the horse goes right. Right rein on the neck means the horse goes left.

Pull back gently for stop, kick your heels into his sides to go faster and hang on to the horn if you feel safer that way," Jake instructed. "Don't drop the reins or he might trip over them and fall."

It was a lot to remember. Elizabeth glanced overhead. The moon was out in all its glory to light their way. "Where are we going?"

"Beats me." The man shrugged. "Bobby?"

"Huh?"

"Where are we going?" Jake asked.

"I thought we'd ride out to the old homestead," the young man announced. "We can follow the fence line to the lake and then back home again."

Jake frowned. "You sure?"

"I've brought something for us to drink," Bobby said. "It'll be great."

Jake looked at Elizabeth and raised his eyebrows. "Are you all right?"

"So far, but we haven't moved yet." Elizabeth smiled, feeling a little more comfortable knowing that Jake was watching out for her.

"We'll take it slow," he promised. "Most of the time I'll be right beside you."

She was surprised at how wonderful that sounded.

"Let's go," Jake continued. "Give him a little nudge and get him to walk."

"Okay." Elizabeth took a deep breath and touched her heels to Rocket's sides. Nothing happened, which was comforting. Obviously this horse wasn't raring to go anywhere in a hurry. She tried again, and said, "Okay, Rocket, here we go," and the horse took two steps forward beside Jake's. *Victory.* Elizabeth wanted to turn to make sure Amy and Bobby were following, but she didn't dare take her attention off the horse.

Or her thoughts off the cowboy next to her.

All that rugged Western charm was what had gotten her in trouble in the first place.

She was determined to resist, but she was also determined to stay on the horse no matter how dark the sky or how sore her thighs.

"Quite a moon," Jake said.

"Yes." Elizabeth realized this horseback-by-moonlight plan was actually as romantic as Amy had predicted, which meant nothing tonight was going to be easy.

HE WAS going to kiss her if it killed him. Jake was tired of riding, of making small talk about horses and fences and the size of the moon. At least ten yards behind them, Amy and Bobby chattered softly together, no doubt planning how to ditch the old folks for some privacy.

Hell, Jake couldn't wait. He glanced toward Elizabeth for the ten thousandth time and wondered what the hell the woman was thinking. They weren't exactly strangers, though she sure put on a good show. If he had to call her Ms. Comstock again he'd just as soon toss her, and her cute little behind, into the water trough.

"Is that it?" Elizabeth asked, and Jake looked over to see her pointing to the dark outline of the old cabin, with its sagging roof and lopsided porch.

"That's it. Where the Calhouns began homesteading in the eighteen hundreds."

"Are we going to go in?" Elizabeth asked.

"Yes, ma'am," Bobby replied, reining in his horse next to Elizabeth's. "I thought Amy should see how the ranch started out."

Jake knew that wasn't the only reason for this trip back to the past. Any red-blooded Texan would have more on his mind tonight than history.

Amy's voice came through the darkness. "I can't wait."

"In that case," Jake said, urging his horse forward. "We'd better get going." The future Mrs. Calhoun was about to see what the past Mrs. Calhouns endured for love. And for a roof over their heads.

"Is it safe?" Elizabeth asked a few minutes later, before stepping foot on the porch stairs.

"Wait," Jake warned, shining the flashlight on the worn boards. "Let me go first to make sure."

"Thanks."

Over by the horses Bobby was busy kissing Amy, so Jake kept Elizabeth's attention on him, which was exactly where he wanted it. He trod carefully on the stairs, even though he had stopped here two weeks ago and found the place in good shape. He made a big deal of shining the flashlight on the boards and sweeping the beam of light across the porch. Then he held out his hand.

Elizabeth took it without hesitating, and Jake grasped warm, delicate fingers in his. He felt the shock in his gut, though he thought he'd prepared himself for the reaction.

"What?" she asked when he stopped moving.

"Nothing," Jake lied. "You're perfectly safe."

But he didn't release her hand, and she didn't tug it away. He supposed she was still unsure about entering the old place, and he couldn't say he blamed her. It looked a hell of a lot worse than it was, but inside he would light a lantern and, if Bobby remembered the saddlebag, there would be something to drink.

"Is it locked?"

"This is Calhoun land." Jake lifted the metal latch and swung the small wooden door open. "Stay beside me," he told Elizabeth, just in case she had any ideas about dropping his hand and moving more than a few inches away. He liked how close she stood to him, the faint scent of lavender that clung to her hair, the softness of her hand he remember being on his—

"Jake!" Bobby clomped onto the porch. "You gonna get a light on or what?"

"We're looking," he said, as Elizabeth tugged her hand out of his and took a couple of careful steps away. He swung the flashlight toward where the lantern hung, then set it in the middle of the square pine table. It didn't take Amy and Bobby long to join them or to open some expensive-looking cognac and pour some into four tiny glasses.

The kid handed out the drinks, then lifted his in a toast. "To your long stay in Texas, ladies."

Amy smiled and leaned over to kiss his cheek. "That's sweet," she said, then turned to her aunt. "Isn't that sweet?"

"Very," Elizabeth said flatly. She took a sip of the drink. "This is wonderful."

"Guaranteed to take the aches and pains away," Bobby declared.

"Is that a promise?" Elizabeth asked.

"Yes, ma'am. Jake and I have had experience with long days in the saddle and we know how your thighs are gonna feel later on tonight."

Jake choked on the cognac, despite the fact that his boss had opened the real expensive stuff, the bottle that his grandfather had saved for a special occasion. When he caught his breath he turned to Bobby. "You might want to rephrase that, kid."

Bobby thought for a second, then grinned at the ladies. "'Course, *I'm* not feeling anyone's thighs tonight."

Elizabeth smiled, which made Jake wish once

again that they were alone. "Don't worry. I knew what you meant the first time." She gazed around the one-room cabin. "So this is where your family began the ranch."

"I come from a long line of stubborn Texans," Bobby declared, putting his arm around Amy's shoulders. "Once we get set on something we don't quit."

"I can see that." Elizabeth took another drink. "The women in your family must have worked awfully hard, cooking the meals and taking care of the children in such a small home."

History again, Jake thought with disgust. When she should be in his arms and he should be reminding her that what they had last February they could have again. "We should start back," he said, setting his empty glass on the table.

"I wanted to show Amy the outhouse," Bobby said, tugging the young woman toward the door.

"Why?"

"Because I've never seen one before," Amy said, looking like she'd been deprived of something terrific.

Jake waved them on. No one stayed long in an outhouse, especially a dark one. "We'll wait by the horses."

"Amy—"

"We'll only be a minute, Aunt B," her niece interrupted. "I just want to see it but not go inside."

Elizabeth sighed and held out her glass. "Could I have some more of that?"

"Yes, ma'am." Jake poured another generous helping for both of them. "I never heard of anyone wanting to see an outhouse before."

"They'll use any excuse to be alone," she said, taking the glass. "Thank you."

"They're in love."

"They're in lust," she countered. "There's a difference."

"Yes." Lust was strangers in a hotel room. Love was weddings and kids and no turning back. "But there's nothing wrong with it."

"Of course there is." She sounded sad. "I am so embarrassed about that night."

"You shouldn't be."

"No?" She turned her face to his, her serious gaze focused on his eyes. "Having sex with a stranger isn't something to be embarrassed about? Of course it is."

He put down his empty glass and took her face between his hands. Her skin was like satin against his callused fingers. "There's no shame in touching you," he whispered, running one thumb gently across her lips when she would have opened her mouth to protest.

"Shh," he told her, stepping closer. He bent his head and touched his mouth to hers. He'd meant to be cautious so she wouldn't back away from him, but the instant his lips touched hers he knew that careful was impossible. Stopping was impossible, too, he realized. Just as before.

Because Elizabeth's lips were warm and sweet and opening for him. Because Elizabeth's hands were on his forearms, as if she couldn't decide whether to keep him from leaving or to push him away. He continued to hold her face while he tasted her mouth, felt her melting against his lips and tongue, knew the heat was rising fast. Faster than he remembered.

Amy's laughter forced Jake to remember where he was, a rough cabin much different than the luxurious hotel room with its king-size bed and smooth sheets and room service from which to order turkey sandwiches and chocolate cake at midnight.

Jake released Elizabeth, though he thought it would kill him. He was surprised that his hands didn't shake when he dropped them from her face. Chatter between Amy and Bobby came from around back. "They're heading toward the horses," Jake said, his voice sounding throaty as he spoke.

"We'd better go." She tucked loose strands of hair behind one ear, and her fingers shook.

Jake took the trembling hand and put it to his lips. "It's going to be all right, Beth," he told her, using the Chicago nickname deliberately.

Her smile was lopsided. "I'm supposed to be chaperoning my niece and look what happens."

"Proves you're human," he said, dropping her hand for a moment while he extinguished the lamp. He put the cognac and glasses in the saddlebag before taking her hand in his once again. "There. Chores are done."

"Wait," she said, planting her feet when he took one step toward the door. "What happened to us last winter was...very unusual. We were both in a strange situation and it just...escalated. And I'm sorry."

"I'm not."

"I didn't come to Texas for sex, Jake."

"I know you didn't, sweetheart," he said, leading her toward the cabin door. "But while you're here, you really should keep an open mind."

Her laughter surprised him, but then again, he should have expected the unexpected from Elizabeth. Jake whistled as they headed across the field, mostly to warn Bobby that they were about to have company. It was awfully quiet over by the grove of trees, and Jake figured Bobby was taking advantage of the privacy.

He'd sure taught the boy well!

"TOMORROW," Elizabeth called over the sound of running bathwater. "We're getting out of here tomorrow. No matter what."

Amy stood at the bathroom door and tried to sound comforting. "You'll feel better after you've

soaked those sore muscles, Aunt B, I just know it."
She also knew that Bobby was on the brink of pro-
posing—this time for real—and she wanted to be in
the same state when he did, not on the other end of
a telephone.

"Muscles have nothing to do with it," Elizabeth
insisted. Amy heard the water shut off, then a contented sigh as her aunt lowered herself into the tub.

"Better?" Amy asked.

"Umm. Remind me never to get on a horse
again."

"It wasn't that bad," Amy said, trying to contain
her laughter. Her thighs felt as if she'd been riding
for a week, but she wasn't going to admit to her aunt
that ranch life didn't suit her perfectly. She would
never tell anyone that she was afraid of horses, that
she'd pretended interest in an outhouse to delay
getting back on the animal's back, that Bobby's
kisses were the only reason she'd enjoyed the moonlight ride.

Surely every future bride had some misgivings
about her upcoming change of lifestyle. But this was
something that she couldn't discuss with her aunt.

"Amy, are you still out there?" Elizabeth wondered.

"Yes." Amy remembered she was supposed to
take Pookie outside one more time before bed, so
she walked over to the bed and scooped the sleepy
animal into her arms. "I'm taking Pookie right

now," she said, anticipating her aunt's next question.

"Thanks. I'm not sure I could walk down the stairs and then back up again tonight," Elizabeth admitted.

Amy wasn't so sure she could manage, either, but she kept her complaints to herself. She was going to be a good ranch wife if it killed her, and besides, Bobby was going to walk with her in front of the house while Pookie found just the right spot in which to do his business. If they were lucky, Pookie would take his time.

The little dog nuzzled into her neck while Amy waddled down the hall to the stairs. Bobby was going to propose, she was going to say yes, and Aunt Elizabeth would finally see that her niece had grown up into a woman able to make her own decisions.

Her own *good* decisions.

"Aunt B is going to have to stay for the wedding," she whispered into Pookie's ear. "And you can carry the rings."

7

ELIZABETH didn't want to dream of kisses. Or cowboys. Or the way the moon highlighted the planes of Jake's handsome face as he'd bent down to kiss her three hours and twenty-six minutes ago.

Very much the same way he'd kissed her that first time in Chicago. There had been brandy that night, too, warming her throat and making her content with the world, even though the part of the world she could see from the hotel window was nothing but blank snowy white.

"Beth?" he'd said, coming to stand behind her as she'd looked into the snowy night. Only a few headlights broke up the darkness. He'd put his large hands on her shoulders and she'd leaned back just a little, to show she didn't mind. But she'd wondered if she'd gone a little bit crazy, especially when he'd turned her toward him and she went right into his arms without a second thought.

He'd held her face so softly. And he'd kissed her, a tentative touch that turned quickly into something else, something as fierce and overwhelming as the storm outside the window. Something that could overturn her careful schedule as easily as a winter blizzard.

They'd had such fun being snowbound together. He'd told her stories of Texas; she told him of her students, the best and the worst. He'd rechecked into his room and given her the key. But of course she'd invited him up to the room for coffee and brandy. Neither one of them wanted to be alone, and it was only polite to share the room until evening forced them to separate. She hadn't expected to feel so attracted to the cowboy, to wonder what it would be like to touch him. To be touched by him.

Elizabeth wondered if she should blame the storm for this rising sexual tension in the room, if fate and the weather had forced them together to see what would happen.

All Elizabeth knew was that she felt just a little bit crazy. And, when this extremely appealing man took her into his arms, not so alone.

There were some nights when she hated being alone. No wonder she couldn't sleep, Elizabeth realized, struggling out of the bed to find Pookie. She lifted the snoring dog out of his bed and put him on hers, then got under the sheet once again. Pookie nestled against her, content. And Elizabeth envied him.

Tomorrow she would put her foot down, gather the plane tickets and make plans to leave. She had to go home before she was tempted to sleep with someone other than a six-pound Shih Tzu.

"IT'S OFFICIAL," Bobby announced to the men at breakfast in the bunkhouse. "I'm really getting married."

"No kidding?" Marty grinned. "That's damn good news, Calhoun. But you said that weeks ago."

"This time it's real."

Shorty didn't look up from his eggs. "Good for you. Now someone pass the pepper down here." Bobby leaned over and tossed the pepper shaker to the other end of the table, where Jake caught it and handed it to the older man.

"Does her aunt know?" Jake asked.

"Amy's going to tell her this morning," Bobby said, glancing to the clock on the microwave. "Probably in about an hour."

Jake leaned back in his chair and ignored the pile of eggs on his plate. He'd cooked them thinking he was hungry, but this information was more important. "And you think her aunt's going to approve?"

The kid shrugged. "Dunno."

"But wasn't that the reason your girlfriend brought her aunt out to the ranch?" Jake asked.

"Yep. Aunt B sure enjoyed those antique stores you took her to. What are you doing today?"

"I have tickets to the grange quilt show," Jake muttered, wishing he could take Elizabeth back to the old cabin for a couple of hours. That woman had kissed him back and then hadn't spoken another word all the way to the ranch. He'd give a hell of a lot right now to know what she was thinking. She sure wasn't leaving today, he knew that.

"Quilt show?" Shorty guffawed. "You're gonna spend your day off at a quilt show?"

"Beats cleaning out a barn," Jake answered, thinking of the work he had to do on his own place. One day a week never gave him enough time to make much progress, that was certain.

Shorty rose and picked up his empty dishes. "Does that mean I have to take care of that dog again?"

"I'll make it worth your while. Marty's mother doesn't want him in the house when no one's with him." Jake recalled Mrs. Martin complaining this morning that Bobby and Amy were up to no good last night under the guise of walking the dog. She also said the dish towels were a disgrace, the hot water heater was set too low, and she was certain Pookie had taken liberties with the rug by the back door, but she couldn't prove it.

"Twenty bucks," Shorty declared.

"Just don't lose him this time," Bobby warned. "It took us an hour to find the little guy yesterday."

"How the hell was I s'posed to know he liked to hide in beds?" He tossed the dishes in the sink. "Whose turn is it to clean up?"

"Mine," Jake said, because it was futile to expect their love-crazed boss to do an assigned chore. That was another thing that would change with a wedding, and Jake couldn't wait. "When do you plan on saying 'I do'?"

"Soon," the kid said with a grin. "Very, very soon."

"Remember what I said," Jake warned, hoping the boy would behave himself. "You don't want her aunt to think you brought Amy here just to...well, you know what I mean."

"Hey." The kid had the nerve to grin at him. "I'm getting married *soon*, Jake. We're going to town to pick out a ring."

"Nothing's open on Sunday."

"I called and begged and Joey said he'd open up the store just for me right after church."

Shorty stopped at the door and turned around to stare at Bobby. "You're going to church?"

"Not me. Joey. He owns his father's jewelry store now and he said he'd give me a good deal on a ring."

Jake retrieved his plate and picked up his fork. He'd rather eat cold eggs than see Elizabeth's reaction when she heard there was going to be a wedding after all. He thought he'd better wait a while before heading over to the main house, at least until the fireworks were over.

"YOU STILL want to go?"

Elizabeth helped herself to another piece of buttered toast and sat down at the kitchen table. "Yes, Jake. Why wouldn't I?"

"Uh, no reason." Then she didn't know, Jake figured. Or she'd be packing up to leave instead of munching toast as if she didn't have a care in the world.

"Do you think any of the quilts on display will be for sale?"

He shrugged. "I don't know. Maybe. Sometimes at the fair there's a quilt raffle. You're shopping?"

"I might. As a souvenir of my trip."

He stared at her across the table. Today she wore some kind of blue dress that showed off her shoulders and neck and looked real good on her. "I thought you might want to go riding again," he teased. He'd seen the way she'd winced when she sat down in her chair.

"No, thank you. But it wasn't as frightening as I thought it would be." She took a deep breath and looked him straight in the eye. "I owe you an apology."

"What for?" He wondered what she'd do if he leaned across the table and kissed her. An intriguing toast crumb clung to her upper lip, which she licked and retrieved. Jake stared, fascinated.

"For being such a pain in the rear," she said. "You've been very nice to us, to me, this weekend and I hope I wasn't rude to you."

Jake cleared his throat and thought about getting her alone again. "You weren't."

"None of this is your fault," she continued. "You didn't know that Amy goes through stages as easily as she changes her shoes and—"

"Come home with me," he interrupted, unsure how much longer he could keep from lifting her across the table and setting her on his lap.

"What?"

He opened his mouth to repeat himself as Mrs. Martin entered the kitchen, her arms loaded with groceries.

"You two still here?" She arched her brows and frowned at him.

Which of course they were. Jake nodded.

"We'll be out of your way in a few minutes." Elizabeth hurried to explain. "We're going off to the quilt show in town."

Mrs. Martin nodded her approval. "Take the boss and the girlfriend with you. They've been kissing in the living room for the past fifteen minutes."

Lucky boss.

Elizabeth jumped up and, stopping to put her cup and plate in the sink, headed to stop her niece from sure disaster, Jake assumed.

"I warned you about these kinds of shenanigans," Mrs. Martin grumbled. "Marty's doin' nothing but mooning around after those twins. He'd be better off picking one or the other and settling down himself."

Jake was tired of discussing other people's love lives. Bobby and Marty were old enough to take care of themselves, old enough to make their own mistakes and pick their own women.

Just as he was overdue to claim his.

And claim her he would, as soon as she'd seen the Texas Textiles display at the grange hall. After all, how long could it take to see a quilt show?

ELIZABETH thought later that she should have seen it coming, but she'd been so pleased with her new quilt she'd missed all the signs that something else was going on besides basic life-on-the-ranch activity when Amy and Bobby were waiting to greet the car.

"Where's Pookie?" It was her first question when she saw Amy holding hands with Bobby and there was no little dog in sight.

"Taking a nap with Shorty," Bobby explained. "Uh, Ms. Comstock, we have—"

"Something to tell you," Amy finished for him, holding out her hand.

"What?" Elizabeth hugged the flower garden quilt she had purchased. She wanted to unfold it and examine every little piece of pastel hexagon fabric. She wanted to picture it on the foot of her Cape Cod bed tomorrow night, ready for foggy nights when a quilt was needed in order to stay warm.

"It's official," Amy said, wriggling her fingers. "Now that you've met him and everything, I said yes."

"Said yes," Elizabeth echoed, still holding the quilt to her despite the heat of the late afternoon sun. They'd been gone for hours, because it had taken her such a long time to make up her mind between the flower garden, double wedding ring and appliquéd pansy quilts. Blue, pink, pale green or lavender...none of the choices were easy. "Said yes to what?"

"Marriage, Aunt B," Amy announced and, ignoring the bundle of fabric, threw herself into her aunt's arms. "I knew you'd love him."

"Oh, dear." It was the only thing Elizabeth could think of to say. She looked past Amy's shoulder to the young cowboy. He grinned uncertainly. "Congratulations," Elizabeth told him. Maybe it would be a long engagement, long enough for them both to come to their senses.

"When?" Jake asked, looking as if he wanted to be anywhere else.

"We're getting married on the Fourth of July," Bobby announced.

"*This* year?"

"Yes, ma'am."

Jake caught the quilt as it dropped, leaving Elizabeth free to finally notice the sparkling diamond engagement ring on Amy's finger. "Are you sure about this?"

"Yes, Aunt B. Really, really sure."

Elizabeth looked over toward Jake, who was busy shaking Bobby's hand. He turned to meet her gaze, but instead of looking sympathetic or triumphant he stood there, her quilt bundled up underneath his arm, and met her gaze.

"You want to go out for dinner?" Jake asked, as if he understood her urge to escape. He even went to the passenger door and opened it for her.

"Sure," Elizabeth heard herself reply.

"But Aunt B, we've got to plan a wedding!" Amy wailed. "You can't leave *now*."

She didn't want to plan a wedding. She wanted to have dinner with the cowboy and pretend that she was getting on a plane. Maybe she really *would* get on a plane. Elizabeth turned away from her niece and returned to Bobby's wide, comfortable, airconditioned Cadillac. Jake tossed the quilt in her lap, then shut the door.

Elizabeth remembered to wave goodbye.

"IT'S LIKE THIS," Jake began, after taking a good long drink of cold beer. To his surprise Elizabeth had ordered one, too, and seemed happy to be drinking it. The Steak Barn wasn't crowded late Sunday afternoon, but the waitress had seated them at a small table in the corner anyway, which suited Jake just fine. He shifted in his chair and accidentally brushed Elizabeth's knees with his own, and sent shock waves right to his groin. He tried not to wince, but it wasn't easy. Looking at her wasn't easy. Smelling her perfume—he thought it might be lavender but he wasn't sure—wasn't easy, either.

Remembering making love to her wasn't real easy, either.

"What's like what?" she asked.

She was looking at him with those beautiful eyes of hers. For a moment he forgot what he was talking about. "This wedding thing." He cleared his throat. "Bobby's never wanted to get married until now, and I have to tell you that we're all pretty damn pleased that he wants to settle down." Jake took another drink. "What I want to know is why you're so against it?"

"They're too young."

"Lots of couples are. What else?"

"I don't think Amy knows what she's getting into." She leaned back to allow the waitress to deposit a basket of tortilla chips and a crock of salsa in the middle of the table.

"Does anyone?"

Elizabeth didn't appear to have an answer for that one, so Jake took advantage of her silence. "Bobby's in love."

"And so, probably, is Amy. But it's not enough."

He frowned. "Why not?"

"They're too different. How on earth is Amy supposed to be a ranch wife?"

"What's wrong with being a ranch wife?"

"Nothing, if you have some idea what it's going to entail."

"Which is?"

"Cleaning and cooking and living far away from town and babies and—"

"You have something against babies?"

"No, of course not, but—"

"There are housekeepers for the rest of it, you know, and Bobby can afford to hire 'em." He didn't tell her that Bobby couldn't hang onto them, but that would change after the wedding, too. "And there are cars and trucks to take you to town, which is only about thirty minutes from here, forty if you drive the speed limit."

"So, if this is all so easy, why haven't *you* married?"

Jake couldn't think of one good reason. Except the truth. "I've been busy taking care of the Dead Horse ranch, that's why. And as soon as Bobby settles down, he can take care of it himself."

"But then what will you do?"

"I have a place nearby. And I sure wouldn't mind spending my time working it." He helped himself to a tortilla chip dipped in the hottest salsa in the county and wondered what Elizabeth would say if he asked her again to come home with him.

"Instead of baby-sitting Bobby Calhoun," she said, coming to the right conclusion.

"Yep. Be careful with the salsa. It's probably hotter than you're used to," he warned, taking a quick drink of beer to cool his throat. If he could cool off the rest of him he'd be in better shape. He noticed she took his advice. The waitress came to the table to take their order, so Jake waited until she scurried off to the kitchen before getting back to the subject of their conversation. "Look," he said. "I know you don't want the kids to get married, but I don't think there's much you can do to stop it."

"Accept the inevitable, you mean."

"Yep."

"In the past couple of years my niece has thought she was an artist, which meant living in Italy, and then she was sure she was meant to be an actress. Don't even ask me what Los Angeles is like," Elizabeth said, pausing to take a sip of her drink. "Last February Amy had become involved with a rock band that left her broke and stranded in the middle of Illinois, which was how I ended up in the Chicago airport."

"Lucky for me," he interjected. But Elizabeth didn't seem to have heard him.

"And now she pictures herself as a cowgirl. Do you see the problem here?" Elizabeth frowned at him, but Jake didn't mind. At least she was talking to him, even if this wasn't going as well as he'd planned.

"Not really," he admitted. "She seems like a nice enough kid, much better than the—" He stopped, realizing he could get in trouble if he wasn't careful.

"The other girls Bobby's dated?" Elizabeth finished for him. "Mrs. Martin told me."

"There are no secrets on the Dead Horse," Jake declared. "Not as long as Mrs. Martin's around." He leaned forward and wished like hell that they were alone. He should never have started talking about Bobby and this damn wedding in the first place. "Honey, all I want is a truce."

"You want a *wedding*."

He wanted a life. "You can't protect that little niece of yours forever, Beth. One of these days you're going to have to let go."

"Which is none of your business," the woman he wanted to take to bed tonight declared, and not too softly, either.

So much for the truce.

SHE KNEW she shouldn't drink when she was with him. Hadn't she blamed the brandy or cognac or whatever it was for the night she spent in bed with a stranger?

"I shouldn't drink." She managed to explain when dizziness made her grab onto Jake's arm as they crossed the restaurant's parking lot to the Cadillac. "Especially when you're around."

"You had two beers," Jake said, putting one very strong arm around her waist so she wouldn't fall.

"One and a half."

"And a steak dinner," he added. "So you're not drunk, Beth. It's more likely the heat. Once you get in the car with the air-conditioning on you'll be fine." He managed to unlock the car and open the passenger door without letting go of her. Well, Elizabeth decided, whatever made her dizzy also made her too aware of his fingers on her waist. And when he guided her to the seat his forearm ever so briefly brushed her breasts.

She was sure he'd done it deliberately, but she didn't actually mind. Not enough to protest or pull away. The sensations sweeping along her skin weren't exactly unpleasant.

Just overwhelming.

"Excuse me," Jake said, moving his arm. Then, still leaning over her as he stood half in, half out of the car, he said, "To hell with this."

When his mouth came down on hers it was as if she'd kissed him a thousand times and could kiss him ten thousand more, if she could just stay in this car. He braced one arm on the seat above her shoulder, the other on the seat next to her thigh. And he continued to kiss her until Elizabeth grew dizzy again, though this time from sheer desire and not the stifling Texas temperature.

She lifted her arms and curled them around his neck while his tongue did lovely things to the inside of her mouth. Somehow she managed to inch toward the steering wheel, giving Jake room to ease onto the seat and free both hands. Having him next to her certainly heated things up.

She didn't know why or how he had this effect on her, but her normally controllable body disintegrated into a quivering mass of sexual awareness whenever he looked at her.

And touched her.

And kissed her in a way that said, "I'm taking you to bed now."

When his hand tangled with her dress hem and connected with her bare thigh, Elizabeth knew she was in trouble. Her first reaction to such an intimate touch was relief, followed by a sheer delightful physical sensation. She forgot she was in a parking lot somewhere in Texas, forgot the sun had yet to set and give them the privacy of darkness, forgot all those promises she'd made to herself about abstinence and propriety and self-control.

His lips dropped to her neck, his fingers skimmed her thigh and higher, to graze the silk underwear she'd foolishly worn on a hot day. His thumb dipped beneath the elastic and touched—

"Damn, Jake, what do you think you're doing?" a male voice asked.

Elizabeth opened her eyes at the same time Jake untangled himself from her clothing and peered around to see Bobby Calhoun staring at him.

"Seat belt was stuck," Jake explained in a gruff voice.

Bobby's jaw hung open, as if he couldn't believe what he just witnessed. "It does that sometimes," he agreed.

Elizabeth felt her face turn red and, as Jake left the seat to stand between her and the car door, tried to rearrange her clothing.

"Were you looking for us?" Jake asked Bobby.

"Yeah. Uh, I just dropped Amy off at the drugstore. She wanted to look at those bridal magazines to get ideas for the wedding. So I thought I'd drive through town and see if you two were still having dinner somewhere."

"We were," Jake said. "We're on our way home."

"Uh, yeah," he said, peering around Jake to stare at Elizabeth again. "I can see that."

"You'd better get back to your fiancée," Jake advised, and Bobby turned and hopped into his truck. Within seconds he'd left the parking area and headed south along Main Street, leaving Jake standing by the car. Jake ducked his head to smile at Elizabeth.

"That was a close call," he said.

"It's what we get for behaving like that in a public place."

"We can go back to my house," he suggested. "I could show you my quilts." The expression in his eyes was one she'd seen before.

Pure unadulterated lust.

Which only meant one thing to Elizabeth: it was time to get out of Texas.

8

"GIVE ME the ticket," Elizabeth said, blocking Amy's bedroom door. "I'm getting out of here even if I have to steal a horse and ride all the way to Dallas."

Amy pulled the covers over her head and nestled deeper into the pillows. "Umph." It was her only response, which Elizabeth expected. Amy had never been a morning person. It wasn't a trait that ran in the family, especially not at seven o'clock on a Monday morning. Elizabeth had gone to bed early last night in an attempt to avoid her niece and she'd been awake since five. Figuring out what to do had taken a long time, especially when Pookie's contented snores kept interrupting her train of thought.

"Don't get up," Elizabeth muttered, crossing the room to her niece's open suitcase on the floor under the window. Within seconds she found her airline ticket, the one with the open return. She was one phone call away from freedom, a long day's travel away from dipping her toes in the frigid Atlantic. "If you want to marry a cowboy then that's what you can do."

"Aunt B? What's the matter?"

Elizabeth clutched her ticket and turned to see her niece struggling to sit up. "Nothing," Elizabeth said, feeling guilty for being such a grouch. It wasn't Amy's fault that her aunt wanted to jump into bed with Jake Johnson. That her aunt *had* jumped into bed with Jake Johnson. "I'm sorry to wake you."

"You're leaving me?" Amy managed to keep her eyes open long enough to make her aunt feel another pang of guilt. "I can't get married without you."

"Sure you can," she countered, unwillingly remembering Jake's words. *One of these days you're going to have to let go.*

"But you're supposed to be my maid of honor," Amy moaned, looking at the ceiling. "And you're the only relative I've got. What kind of a wedding will it be without family?" She struggled once again to sit up and pushed the hair away from her face. "Wouldn't you want me at *your* wedding?"

"Of course I would," Elizabeth said, edging toward the door while her resolve to leave was still strong. "But since I'm not even dating anyone right now I don't think—"

"You were out with Jake," Amy interrupted. "All day. And for dinner, too."

"It's his job to chaperone me."

"Ha!"

"Don't snort, Amy," she said, almost to the door

and two steps away from the end of the conversation. "It's not ladylike."

"Neither is making out in a parking lot, Aunt B." When Elizabeth opened her mouth to protest, Amy put one hand up as if to ward off her words. "Bobby told me. You don't think he believed that silly seat belt explanation, do you?" She grinned. "I'm not the only Comstock woman who likes cowboys, am I?"

"Don't be ridiculous." It was the only thing Elizabeth could think to say before she fled across the hall to the privacy of her room. She sat on her bed and eyed the airline envelope that held her ticket off the ranch and out of Texas. If she thought for a minute that Amy was really getting married, she'd stay for the wedding, of course. She liked weddings.

Pookie stretched his front paws toward her thigh and yawned, so Elizabeth obediently scratched his ears. "I hear you like cowboys, too," she told him. "You little traitor."

Pookie tipped over on his back so she could rub his fat belly, which was another morning ritual. "She's not really getting married," Elizabeth told the dog. "I'm sure it will never happen."

WANTING HER was killing him. No lie. Jake wondered how much longer he could survive sleepless nights. When he did fall asleep, he dreamed of making love to Elizabeth. The solution, of course, was getting Elizabeth back in his bed. And soon. Jake poured himself another cup of coffee and watched the sun rise over the main ranch house. He hoped like hell that she was lying awake thinking of him. He sure didn't want to be miserable all by himself.

For the life of him, Jake couldn't figure out why she was causing so much trouble. The damned woman was determined to act like they'd never met each other before, yet she'd been all heat and softness in the car. Two more minutes and they would have been in the back seat together, which was no way for mature adults to behave, come to think of it.

If it had been dark it would have been possible, though.

The woman wanted him. Maybe just as much as he wanted her. Now that was something.

February wasn't that long ago, and Jake knew they both remembered exactly what had happened. And that it was going to happen again.

"I *quit*." With that statement Mrs. Martin untied her apron and folded it into a neat pile on the kitchen counter. "There's no way I'm putting up with this."

Elizabeth grabbed a handful of paper towels. "Please, Mrs. Martin, I'm sure it won't happen again."

"Not sure enough for me, thank you." The woman huffed. "There's a roast in the oven for dinner, but you'll be wanting to put some potatoes in to bake about an hour before you're ready to eat."

"We'll keep a better eye on him," Elizabeth promised. "And besides, I'm leaving—"

"That's what your niece said last time." Mrs. Martin rinsed a knife and dropped it in the sink while Elizabeth hurriedly sopped up the rest of the quarter-size puddle in the corner and tried to think what to say to stop Mrs. Martin from walking out the door. "But you can't watch him every minute. There's biscuits, too, for heating."

"Thank you, but—"

"I'd planned on slicing up some fresh tomatoes," Mrs. Martin said, heading past the table toward the back door. "There's plenty in the garden."

"He gets nervous, that's all, especially when he hears loud noises." Elizabeth tried to explain, not that Mrs. Martin was listening.

Pookie sat in his bed and watched Elizabeth clean up his latest mess. His ponytail hung to one side, his face needed a good scrubbing and he was coated with a layer of Texas dust. Even the dog had been spending too much time with the cowboys.

"Hmmph," Mrs. Martin said, brushing past Jake as he started to enter the kitchen. He didn't seem bothered by the housekeeper's grumpiness. Instead he watched Elizabeth rise from the floor and put the paper towels in the trash, then he leaned against the counter and helped himself to a cup of coffee as the back door slammed shut.

"You're not going to ask what's going on?"

He took a sip of coffee before answering. "I figure Mrs. Martin just quit."

"That's true, but—"

"Because the runt over there messed on her floor again?"

"He's not a runt. And he doesn't mean to be naughty." Elizabeth washed her hands at the sink, then looked around for a dish towel. Not finding one, she used Mrs. Martin's apron to dry her hands.

"No," the cowboy said, eyeing the dog and looking more amused than he had a right to. "Shorty doesn't seem to mind having him around. Maybe Mrs. Martin would come back if we sent Pook here to live in the bunkhouse for the rest of your stay."

"No," she said. "I'd worry about him too much. I'd be afraid the cowboys would forget he was around and step on him." And there was no way she was going to admit that the little dog kept her company at night. "And anyway, I'm going to—"

"I can see your point," Jake admitted, as he and Pookie looked at each other. "None of the men are going to carry him around like you do." He turned to Elizabeth. "Well, don't worry about Mrs. Martin. That's the fourth or fifth time she's quit being housekeeper around here. We'll figure out something." He glanced toward the kitchen table and frowned. "What is that?"

"My suitcase." It was a completely unnecessary reply, Elizabeth realized. This man had the ability to keep her off balance and turn her into a babbling idiot. "That's what I was trying to tell you."

He arched one eyebrow as he looked at her. "So you've decided to move in with me."

She almost laughed, but settled for what she hoped was a ladylike smile. "Not quite."

He stepped closer and set his coffee cup on the counter. "What about the wedding? I'm surprised you're not staying for the big day."

"And I'll be surprised if it takes place," she said. He was only a foot away but he radiated enough sexual awareness to make her skin tingle. She made a big deal out of folding the apron. "I had this same conversation with Amy this morning."

"Did you," Jake murmured, reaching for one of the blue ties that hung from the bundle in her hands. He tugged on it, and Elizabeth didn't let go. Instead she allowed him to pull her closer. "That's better."

She knew exactly why it was better when he dipped his head and touched her lips with his. Within seconds they were mouth to mouth, tongue to tongue, an instant conflagration of heat and longing. She was against that wonderfully hard chest and, lower, against another intriguing hardness. She heard him groan, felt his hands run down her spine to cup her buttocks and hold her close against him.

It was all she could do to stay on her feet.

And then she didn't, because he'd taken her by the waist and lifted her onto the counter, which made it easy to wrap her arms around his neck and lean into his kiss. Her sundress was over her knees, which were soon parted to allow Jake to stand closer to her. All that heat generated from two specific places. And both those places, Elizabeth realized with some degree of fascination, were touching.

Except for a scrap of silk and a zipper.

"What are we doing?" she managed to say when she paused for breath. His eyes were level with hers, and he looked just as stunned. And just as ready to head back to bed.

"Making love on the counter." His rough-skinned hands swept slowly up the tops of her thighs.

"We can't," Elizabeth managed to say, but his thumb hit a spot that made her jump.

"You want to," he said, tickling her neck with his lips as his fingers brushed the elastic edge of her panties.

"This is going to be embarrassing," she warned. "Amy won't sleep forever and Bobby must be—"

"Checking on the horses," he finished for her, but he removed his hands from under her dress and pulled down the hem. Then he put his palms flat on the counter on either side of her hips and held her gaze. "This has got to stop."

She didn't expect to feel so disappointed. "I agree. If you'll ask someone to drive me to the airport—"

He swore, then apologized. "You're not making

this easy," he said, frowning. "Take a ride with me."

"Not unless it's to the airport, and even then I don't think it's a good idea that you drive—"

"To my home," he said, ignoring her protests. "Bobby's grandfather left me a real nice piece of property northwest of here. The house isn't much to look at, but it'll do. For now."

"I made plane reservations."

"Cancel them."

"I have to leave."

"Why?"

Good question, she thought. So she wouldn't fall into bed with him again? So she wouldn't embarrass herself once more by her powerful sexual attraction to a man she hardly knew? "Because we seem to keep doing…this," she said, adjusting her dress and attempting to put her knees together.

Jake backed up and let her fuss. "I thought you wanted to stop the wedding." He said it as if he thought she needed reminding.

"I've decided to mind my own business." She hopped off the counter and smoothed her hair in place behind her ears. "You were right. It's time I let Amy live her life."

"That's nice," Amy said, hiding a yawn as she stepped into the kitchen. "And I appreciate it, but why can't you stay and be my maid of honor?"

Because I want to have sex on the kitchen counter with

the groom's foreman, that's why. She didn't dare look over at Jake while she tried to think of an answer. "I can come back for the wedding," Elizabeth promised, knowing it sounded lame.

"Are you leaving because you don't like Bobby?" Jake asked.

"Of course not. I, um, feel a little out of place, that's all."

"We could use a housekeeper," Jake said, picking up the apron from the floor. He grinned at her. "Do you want a job?"

"I'd rather go after Mrs. Martin and apologize some more."

"Where'd she go?" asked Amy.

"Pookie upset her again, so she quit."

"Oh. Why aren't you going to stay and help me plan my wedding?" Amy demanded.

"Yes," Jake drawled. "Why aren't you, Elizabeth?"

"Pookie and I should head home before we cause any more trouble for you here." She hoped it sounded like a noble excuse that no one would argue with. "We've already cost you a housekeeper, and I'm sure there's lots of work for you to do without having to take me to quilt shows and antique shops and out to dinner."

"I haven't minded." Jake gave her a look that said, "Come to bed with me". Elizabeth blushed.

"I'll do it," Amy declared, taking the apron from him and tying it around her waist. "I want to."

"Do what?" Jake said with a blank expression.

"You don't know anything about cooking or cleaning," Elizabeth pointed out.

"I cooked in college, when we had the dorm with the kitchen. And how hard can cleaning be?"

"Bobby's not going to like this," Jake said. "You're a guest."

"Not for long," the young woman declared. "In eight days this will be my home."

Elizabeth realized her mouth was hanging open and quickly pressed her lips together. Amy now saw herself as a ranch wife, which meant there was no way she would allow herself to be talked out of it. "She's right," Elizabeth declared. "She may as well learn what she's getting into."

Amy rolled her eyes. "You make it sound horrible, Aunt B."

"Not horrible," Elizabeth said, blinking away a startling and appealing vision of making breakfast to share with Jake at sunrise. "Just different from what you're used to."

"Now you have to stay," her niece insisted. "So I can prove to you that I can do this. But I can't plan my one and only wedding without your help."

"All right," she said, knowing full well she couldn't deny Amy anything. "I'll help you plan the wedding, but you're on your own in the kitchen."

Elizabeth avoided Jake's look of triumph. The truth was she hated to think of missing Amy's wedding. If it really was going to happen, she wanted to be there. Surely she could manage to keep her clothes on for eight more days.

Less, once Amy realized there was more to getting married than being in love.

"WE CAN WAIT eight more days," Amy declared, turning to kiss her fiancé. He stood behind her at the sink and nuzzled the back of her neck. Somehow he had managed to unzip her jeans while she was washing the dishes. All those pots and pans wouldn't fit into the dishwasher, which was disappointing.

"Eight days?"

"Until our wedding night."

He sighed. "You're killin' me, honey."

"It's only eight days," she assured him. And felt quite virtuous for doing so. "Can you hand me that frying pan over there?"

His hands, which had managed to slide up from her waist to her breasts, slowly left her. Bobby shifted to the right and grabbed the pan. "I'm not sure this is a good idea."

"It's only eight—"

"Not that. This cooking and cleaning thing." Bobby leaned against the counter and watched her scrub dried egg from the pan. The darn stuff stuck like glue to the sides. "I can find another house-keeper."

"Jake said you couldn't."

"Well, he doesn't know everything. I'll bet I could scare up one somewhere."

"Right now you don't need one."

"We will when the babies start coming."

"Babies?" Amy hadn't thought of having babies. At least not right away. Not until she was twenty-nine. Or thirty. Or thirty-five.

"Sure." Bobby winked at her before moving toward the door. "I'm gonna need three or four sons to help me run this place. See you later."

Of course he was only teasing, Amy thought, turning on the water to rinse the soap off the pans before putting them in the dish drainer. She heard the door slam, heard his booted footsteps on the wooden porch floor as he headed to whatever he was doing. For a man who ran a large ranch, Bobby Calhoun seemed to have a lot of free time. She eyed the stack of pots and grabbed a dish towel from its hook by the sink. Maybe she should have asked him to help dry.

"YOU'VE GOT IT BAD, boss," Dusty said, and pulled two bottles of beer out of the bunkhouse refrigerator. He set them on the table and sat down, motioning for Jake to join him.

"Yeah?" Dusty was about his age, but Jake didn't

know any more about the man than that he was an expert on grasslands and one hell of a rider. He'd been here seven years and hadn't uttered one personal sentence, so Jake eyed him with some suspicion as he pulled a chair up to the table.

"Long day." Dusty flicked his bottle cap and tossed it twelve feet to land squarely in the garbage can.

"Sure was." Jake twisted off the cap and set it on the table.

"I heard the kid took the women for a horseback ride."

"Yep." Jake had opted to check fence rather than torture himself with what he couldn't have. "What's the betting up to?"

"Two to one the kid will still be a bachelor on July fifth. You, on the other hand, are running just about fifty-fifty."

"Me?" He should have known they'd bet on anything.

"The men think the auntie's got you hog-tied and ready for roasting."

"Meaning?"

Dusty hummed a few notes of the "Wedding March" and then grinned. "Your days are numbered, Jake. You're a tortured man."

"I've got no argument with the tortured part." He took a healthy swallow of beer. And another one, because he'd sure as hell never thought about getting married. And he said so.

The other cowboy shrugged. "Happens to all of us sooner or later."

Jake had to smile. "Even you?"

"Well, no," he drawled, making Jake chuckle. "I was speaking in a general sense, boss."

"I haven't thought much about marriage," Jake admitted.

"You've been too busy doing Calhoun's work to think about women?"

"I thought about them," he said. "And dated a few from time to time." But no one compared to Elizabeth Comstock. He'd admired her calm demeanor at the airport, enjoyed talking to her more than he'd ever enjoyed talking to a woman before. And talking to women didn't come easy. "But I like this one."

"Yeah. It's pretty obvious." Dusty drained the rest of his beer. "I put my money on you."

"To do what?" Jake eyed the dark-haired cowboy who rarely had this much to say. "Stay a bachelor?"

"Hell, no," he said. "I've got a hundred bucks that says you won't." With that he stood up and tossed the empty bottle in the trash. "Besides, Shorty's crazy about that little dog."

"WELL, THAT WAS easy enough," Amy declared, tossing a dishtowel onto the counter with a great flourish. "I think I might actually be good at this."

"Honey, it was great." Bobby beamed as he covered up the leftover roast beef with plastic wrap. "I can't believe you've never cooked before."

Neither could Elizabeth. The dinner of roasted potatoes, sliced tomatoes, corn and roast beef had been delicious. Mrs. Martin had started it, but Amy was the one who put it together. Forget *Baywatch* and art classes. Maybe her niece had a knack for domesticity, after all.

"Are you two still serious about getting married on the Fourth of July?" she asked, amazed at how young they looked standing together by the refrigerator. Bobby gave Amy a quick hug as he faced her aunt.

"Sure we are," he said. Amy nodded.

"Then we have work to do." She pulled a notepad and pen out of her purse. "I guess we'd better start making lists."

Bobby's face fell. "We were going to the movies."

Amy looked at her watch. "We've got an hour before the show starts, which gives us—how long?"

"Five minutes," Bobby said. "What do you want to do?"

Elizabeth wanted to laugh. Instead she said, "Make a list of wedding guests to call? I think it's too late to send invitations."

"Sure. What else?"

"I'll call my girlfriends," Amy offered. "I know some of them will come. Everyone wants to meet real cowboys."

That's when Jake entered the kitchen. "Who wants to meet real cowboys?"

"Amy's college friends," Elizabeth replied, checking off "guests." "Where are you going to have the wedding?"

"Here," Bobby said.

Jake cleared his throat, and everyone looked at him. "Or in town, at the grange hall. There's fireworks after sundown, so we can all go over to the park after the party."

"So you want to get married in the afternoon?" Elizabeth asked.

"No. Too hot," Jake said. "Maybe later, around six. Then we can have something to eat and dance all night."

"Which brings me to the other things, food and music."

"And I have to get a dress," Amy added. "Something white and long, but not too dressy. Don't you think it should be cotton, like Laura Ashley without the flowers?"

"Flowers," Elizabeth repeated. "What kind of flowers do you want to carry?"

"Something Texan," Amy declared. "I know. Yellow roses!" She tugged Bobby's hand. "Do you think yellow roses are okay?"

Bobby looked at Jake as if to beg for mercy. "We were going to the movies," he said. "Mel Gibson."

His foreman didn't let him down. "You're going to be late if you don't get going."

"That's what I thought." Bobby grabbed Amy's hand and headed toward the door. "Don't worry, Ms. Comstock. Jake here will tell you everything you need to know."

Within seconds they were out the door and Elizabeth was left alone with a sexy cowboy and a sleeping dog.

"It's true," Jake said, pulling up a chair. "I do know a lot of things."

"About weddings?"

"They're probably the same as funerals," he said. "And I've planned enough of those, too."

She pushed the notebook aside. "I can't plan someone else's wedding. It's not right."

"Sure it is." He pulled the notebook toward him and studied the list. "You can get the Steak Barn to cater. Just call Millie in the morning and tell her what you want. They could have a small ceremony here at the house and then party later, at the grange. The whole town will be jumping for the Fourth, so it should be quite a reception."

"Don't forget the fireworks."

"You haven't lived till you've seen it." Jake smiled at her, which made Elizabeth wish he wasn't across the table. "You are going to stay, aren't you?"

Like she had a choice.

9

"WELL, NOW WHAT?" Elizabeth asked, looking at Jake as if he had all the answers.

Now what? He could think of a number of things they could do to fill an evening, especially those that involved taking off their clothes and pretending they were alone in a hotel again.

"I think it's snowing," he said. "Can you hear the wind?"

"No." He could swear he saw the flicker of desire in those lovely green eyes before she looked back down at her list of things to do. That's when he wondered if Dusty was right, if his bachelor days were numbered. And if he wanted them to be. Elizabeth Comstock wasn't the cinnamon-scented maternal ranch woman he'd pictured in his home. No, instead there was that intriguing scent of lavender and the vision of tangled sheets, soft skin and silken thighs.

Which beat the hell out of housekeeping any day.

"Want to take a ride?"

"On a horse or in a car?" She wrote something in the margin before looking at him again.

"Truck."

"I'm getting better at riding," she told him. "Even Bobby said so."

"I believe you, but what I want to show you is too far away."

"Where are we going?"

"Do I have to tell you everything?" Jake held out his hand, which she took, and tugged her to her feet.

Elizabeth hesitated as she neatly stepped around the dog bed. "Can I take Pookie? I don't want to leave him here alone."

"If you want, or I can bring him over to Shorty. I guess he's starting to like the little...guy."

She bent and picked up the dog and his battered little bed. "I'll bring him. I may need a chaperone."

"I'm shaking in my boots," Jake said, and held the door open.

Twenty minutes later he drove her through the open gate and onto the road that led to his place. "You're on Johnson land now," he said, wondering if she would think his pride was an odd thing, considering the modest house in the distance.

"Bobby's grandfather left this whole ranch to you?"

"Yeah. It belonged to his mother's family. They were original homesteaders in this county. It's small compared to the Dead Horse, but it's still big enough to make a living on."

"He must have thought a lot of you," Elizabeth said, gazing at the distant house.

Jake swallowed the sudden lump in his throat and tried to sound casual. "He wanted me close by to watch over his grandson."

Elizabeth gave him a searching look, as if she realized how much he missed the old man. "He liked this ranch?"

"Yes." R.J. kept the house up, though he could easily have had it torn down. He made repairs and acted just like someone lived there. Would live there. "He took good care of everything that was his."

"And now you're doing the same thing," she said, as they quickly approached the faded blue house.

"I try." Except everything that was his consisted of only his horse and his home, and from the deserted look of the place he hadn't done such a great job. He pulled up in front of the house and surveyed the front porch. It looked as if it could use a good sweeping, but then it always did. Without living here permanently he couldn't keep up with the Texas dust.

"Why don't you live here?"

"My job's on the Dead Horse for now, remember? I'll give you the grand tour, though." He shut off the engine and glanced down at the dog asleep at her feet. "Bring Pook in with you."

"I'll hold onto him." She bent over and put him on her lap, then opened the truck door.

"I'm not real worried," Jake said, figuring the dog could take care of business on the way across the yard, which Pook proceeded to do a couple of times after Elizabeth set him down to walk beside her.

Jake took her hand as she started up the steps beside him. Her skin was warm and soft, her fingers curling gently around his as if they were old friends. But they were old lovers instead, and the urge to tug her against him was almost impossible to control. It was all purely physical, he assured himself.

Making love to her once again would take care of everything, would settle his senses into some kind of calm. He hadn't had a woman since February, since she'd left his bed and disappeared from his life. He hadn't wanted anyone else but her, even though common sense had told him he'd never see her again.

To hell with common sense. Jake kept hold of her hand until she pulled away to retrieve Pookie, who had hesitated at the stairs. Elizabeth went back to get the dog.

"He's afraid of stairs," she explained. "I taught him to go up, but sometimes he forgets how."

Jake could believe it, considering that vacant look in the dog's eyes. There was probably a lot that dog forgot he ever knew, which made the dog a heck of a lot smarter than the rancher standing on the porch watching the animal. Jake unlocked the front door and waited for Elizabeth to join him. "He's not exactly a ranch dog, is he?"

She smiled, and his heart stopped beating for the time it took to remember to breathe. "No, I guess not. But he was the perfect dog for an old lady."

"Which you're not," he pointed out, as he pushed the door open and gestured for her to step inside the house.

"He's good company."

"Yeah, you've said that before." Jake followed her into the house and switched on the light to the right of the door frame, illuminating the center hall and the stairs leading to the second story.

"It's beautiful," she said, and for a second he almost believed she really thought so.

"It needs work." He pointed to the room to the right. "Living room," he said. "Runs the length of the house."

"That's a beautiful fireplace." Elizabeth pointed to the stonework that covered the middle section of the far wall.

"The kitchen's on the other side," Jake told her, but he led her into the empty room on the opposite side of the hall. "I guess this was the dining room, but I'm not sure."

"It's a shame no one lives here."

"I've got some stuff in storage, but not much. My mother lived on the Dead Horse and didn't need furniture of her own." He touched Elizabeth's back and guided her through the room, past the long windows that faced the east pasture and through a wide doorway with closets tucked into each side, to the kitchen. "This is the only part of the house I really use."

Elizabeth set Pookie on the tiled floor and walked over to the black iron cookstove with a pipe that went into the stone chimney. "This is amazing," she said, gazing around her. "It looks like something out of a magazine."

"It does?" Jake looked around, seeing nothing fancy in the rectangular room. He was partial to the long table that took up the center space. Rough and stained, it had withstood a hundred years of cooking for ranch hands and families. Pots still hung from ceiling hooks near the stove, and a worn braided rug covered the center of the floor. The window over the sink faced east, the back door led to the kitchen garden and the west windows showed his favorite view, the barn and outbuildings across the yard, the sun low on the horizon.

"I can see why you love it." Elizabeth smiled at him, and he knew it was just about too much to resist.

"Beth," he said, his voice sounding strange and hoarse. He was close enough to touch her, but he didn't. He couldn't bear it if she pulled away, if she broke his heart in this room, in what was to be his home soon.

"Jake," she said, her voice holding a warning note. She didn't move away. Instead she stood there looking at him, a question in her green eyes.

Jake remembered it was exactly the way she'd looked at him those long months ago, while the storm raged outside and snow battered the windows. He had come up behind her and touched her shoulders. She'd turned around and he'd cupped her face and kissed her. And she'd looked at him with that questioning expression, as if to say, "Who are you and how do you do this to me?"

This time he didn't touch her face, which took more self-control than he knew he had. "Beth, honey, do we need a storm?"

She shook her head. "No."

"No, you're not going to kiss me or no, we don't need a blizzard to be together?" She opened her mouth to respond, but he sensed the refusal coming and stopped her. "No, don't say anything. I'm not sure I can take much more rejection." She smiled at his feeble attempt at humor and then looked around for the dog. Pookie lay curled up in the corner in a pile of bath towels.

"Do I get the rest of the tour?"

"Yeah."

They left the dog snoring in the kitchen while Jake led Elizabeth upstairs and showed her the three bedrooms, complete with iron beds and dressers with peeling paint and faded quilts covering the sagging mattresses.

"I guess I'd better start buying new furniture," he said, opening a window to let air cool the stifling second floor.

"You could use new mattresses," she agreed, "but the rest is perfect."

"I'm going to have the floors sanded and refinished."

"Then all you'll need are some throw rugs," she said, helping him open the windows in the largest room, the one he would take for himself when he moved in. It had its own entrance to the bathroom, and one of the previous owners had built in cupboards and shelves along the west wall. He'd stored most of his mother's things in the cedar chest at the foot of the bed. "To match the quilts."

He glanced toward the blue checked quilt that covered the double bed. And then he thought he'd better not look at that bed any more. He could picture Beth waking in this room, reaching for him under the warmth of the covers. "Those aren't the ones I was telling you about. The best are in the chest over there."

"Can I see?"

"Sure." Jake walked over and lifted the lid, Elizabeth close behind him. Lifting the lid brought the fragrance of cedar and the musty smell of clothing stored for a long time. "Help yourself."

She knelt on the floor in front of the chest and lifted out a bundle wrapped in tissue paper. "This is like Christmas," she said, darting a glance his way before unwrapping the tissue to reveal a quilt made of small strips that formed squares. She touched the brown and cream fabrics with reverent fingers and traced the stitching gently. "Your mother did beautiful work."

"Not my mother," he said, sitting on the edge of the bed so he could see her face. Was this how a man in love behaved? "My grandmother and her sisters. She used to say it was all she had of her family."

Elizabeth wrapped the quilt and placed it carefully beside her on the floor before reaching for another bundle. "Are you sure you don't mind?"

He shook his head. "Take all the time you need," he replied. Maybe he was in love with her if he was content to sit here and watch her admire old bedding. If this was what love did to a man, then maybe he should try to get out now, before he did something foolish.

He should make love to her or avoid her, Jake figured, watching Beth's face light up as she unwrapped something yellow and delicate-looking. Somehow he had to put himself out of this misery of wanting her and not having her.

"I think it's a baby quilt," she announced, unfolding the blanket to hold it up to show him.

Jake hadn't thought about babies, but even that possibility didn't make him want to get on his horse and gallop to Mexico. "Do you want children?" he asked.

"Of course. I think this is one of those Lone Star patterns." She studied the design as she held it at arm's length. "I'd like to have at least two. And then Amy would have to be the sensible aunt instead of me."

He could have said, *Marry me.* He could have said, *Stop being so sensible and come to bed.* But he didn't. Instead Jake stood and went over to the window to study the setting sun, just as he had thousands of times before. He might as well face the fact that he'd fallen in love with her from almost the first moment he saw her. How else could he explain not being able to sleep? And when he did, he dreamed of snow and making love...and a chestnut-haired woman who was there when he woke up in the morning.

Jake wasn't an impulsive man, but it took everything he had to keep silent and not embarrass himself. She was an educated woman, a New England woman. She had money and a house on a beach and she was independent and beautiful. What could he offer a woman like that?

He turned from the window and caught her

watching him, so he hooked his thumbs in his pockets and waited for her to hold up another one of his mother's quilts.

"Thank you for showing these to me," Elizabeth said, smiling at him before turning her attention to the trunk.

"No problem." It was all Jake could think to say, walking past her toward the door. Jake needed some air and he needed to get away from that bed. The woman didn't want him, and he'd have to get used to that fact.

He'd been through worse, and he'd get through this, so when Elizabeth turned to him with a question in her eyes, he explained, "I'm going to check on Pook. Close up the chest when you're done."

"GIVE ME just another minute."

"We're supposed to meet everyone for a beer at the Last Chance," Bobby complained, tapping his booted foot on the wooden floor of the town's only drugstore.

"They'll wait," Amy assured him, wondering what the big rush was about. Here she was, responsible now for the family's nutrition and well-being, and he wanted to rush her away from the local cookbooks tucked in between the mystery novels and the how-to books so he could quench his thirst. "I want to find some recipes for tomorrow and then we'll need to go to the grocery store to get the things I need to make them."

"Honey." He put his arm around her shoulders. "Forget about cooking. We can just buy everything at the store. You know, like frozen waffles and a couple of those big chicken pot pies. We've had those before and—"

"No way." She rifled through the quick-bread section of the grange cookbook and thought it looked simple enough. "I want to do it all myself."

"Why?"

Amy thought she'd never seen such a look on a man's face before. She shrugged out of his embrace and handed him the book. "Hold that, will you?"

"Amy Lou, honey, you don't have to cook," Bobby said, still looking puzzled.

"I *need* to cook." She reached for a book in something called the Texas Cooks series. "You just hired me to be the housekeeper, and I intend to do a good job." She handed the book to Bobby and turned to the shelf to select another. "Now I wish I'd taken home ec classes in high school."

"Anything you make will be just fine with me," her fiancé declared.

"You're not the problem," Amy muttered. "Aunt B is."

"Why? What's she done?"

"She doesn't think I'll make a very good ranch wife." Amy quit rifling through the books and pulled one of each off the shelf and placed them on top of the others Bobby patiently held. Everyone expected her to fail. Just because she had a short attention span or something like that. Never mind that she at least tried things, gave it a shot, went for the whole enchilada, as Bobby said once. "I'm going to prove Aunt B wrong. I just know I can do this."

The young cowboy frowned at her, and one slim paperback called *Hot As Hell Chili* fell to the floor. "Honey, you don't have to worry about all this stuff. I love you and you love me. That's all that matters, right?"

Amy picked up the book and didn't bother to hide her frustration as she glanced at her fiancé. "You don't understand, Bobby." She fished her platinum credit card from her purse and headed toward the register. "Love doesn't have anything to do with this at all."

LOVE HAD nothing to do with that night in Chicago, but Elizabeth couldn't stop remembering what had happened between them. Or what might happen again. She didn't know whether to be relieved or disappointed when Jake left her alone in the sparse bedroom. Its double bed and neatly folded bedding seemed an invitation too hard to refuse, especially at sunset. Especially when they were alone.

It was especially hard since she knew what it felt like to take him inside of her, to make love with him several times in one long, memorable night. She sat cross-legged on the floor, an exquisitely stitched wedding ring quilt forgotten in her lap. *Do we need a storm?* Jake had asked only moments ago.

Of course not. All they needed was a few seconds alone. Elizabeth hadn't answered, afraid she would make love with him right there on the kitchen floor and knowing darn well that she had no business behaving that way, no matter what the weather. She was here in Texas to chaperone Amy. She was here to plan a wedding she hoped wouldn't happen. And she was in Jake's future bedroom not because she loved looking at quilts but because she hadn't the sense to stay home and make to-do lists for the Fourth of July wedding ceremony.

And why? Because she hadn't been able to resist being with him. And remembering that one night last winter.

He'd kissed her, his hands on either side of her face. And she'd kissed him back, knowing full well that there would be no turning back. The sexual tension had been building as they had stayed together, talking and laughing in the seclusion of the room. She didn't want to ask him to leave.

And she didn't know how to ask him to stay. She'd never made love to a stranger before. Her limited sexual experiences had been confined to one college boyfriend and a long-ago relationship with a co-worker. Nothing before had felt like this, a combination of passion and longing and trust that made her loop her arms around the cowboy's neck and continue to kiss him until neither one of them could stand upright.

Somehow they managed to get their clothes off, which didn't take long. She tripped over one of the man's cowboy boots, and he chuckled and lifted her onto the bed before tenderly rubbing her stubbed toe.

"Better?" he asked, smiling at her.

Unable to talk, she nodded. And turned back the covers. He flicked off the bedside lamp to leave the room in semidarkness before joining her under the covers. For once in her life, Elizabeth felt she was in the right place at exactly the right time, no matter how crazy it seemed. Or how out of character it was.

"I wonder if the storm has made us crazy," she whispered, turning on her side to face the cowboy. He was all male, with wide bare shoulders and taut chest. His head was propped up by his hand, and the other smoothed a tingling path along her arm and down, to the dip of her waist and the curve of her hip.

"It has," he agreed. "Though I've been in storms before and never done this."

"A blizzard usually means I have the day out of school," she managed to say, though his hand caressed the curve of her buttocks before moving higher once again.

"And what do you do then?" His fingers touched her breast, teasing the nipple with tiny feather-light touches.

"Grade—" his head dipped, his lips laving where his fingers had been "—papers," she whispered, before reach-

ing to pull him closer. He took his time with each breast, kissed the tender skin beneath her earlobes, skimmed her abdomen with strong callused fingers until he found her, moist and ready for him. She wanted him inside of her and didn't know how she could wait much longer. And she told him so.

He left her briefly, and when he returned to the bed she realized he'd remembered the protection she'd foolishly forgotten.

"Thank you," she whispered, as he slid over her.

That made him smile. "You Eastern women are very polite."

Which made her blush.

He leaned forward, positioning himself between her thighs, and she opened her legs to allow him access. He rested his very large, very warm male member against her.

"I don't want to rush you," he said, as if he had to explain.

"You're not." It was just the opposite, she realized. If he didn't take her soon, she was sure to explode in a million pieces if he so much as kissed her again. Her cowboy leaned above her and slanted his mouth across hers in a searching kiss that made her ache with wanting. He kissed her as he slid into her, as she become accustomed to the size of him, as he moved deeper and then withdrew in slow, tantalizing movements. She didn't know how long he made love to her that way, his mouth pressed against hers in a kiss she didn't want to end. He was kissing her

when she climaxed, when her cries sounded against his mouth, while her arms were wrapped tightly around his neck. His thrusts increased, deepening more than she thought possible, until he dragged his mouth away from hers and, his lips against her shoulder, shuddered violently within her.

Elizabeth, nestled deep into the mattress, her body held fast by a contented naked man, prayed the storm would never end.

"THE RUNT'S ASLEEP," Jake announced as he stood in the doorway. No way was he going to enter that bedroom again, not with Beth sitting there by the bed with a lapful of quilts and that wistful expression on her face. "I had an idea—" But he stopped talking when she glanced at him. He could have sworn she looked guilty. "What's the matter?"

"Nothing." She looked at the quilt and started fussing with the material as if she was trying to figure out how to fold it. "I'll be right there."

Jake lingered in the doorway. "I had an idea," he began again, noting that her cheeks were flushed. These Northern women weren't used to Texas weather, he reminded himself. He should be taking better care of her instead of leaving her in a second-story bedroom without even a damn fan to move the air around. What the hell was he thinking?

"What's your idea?"

"Pick out one of the quilts for Bobby and your

niece. I'll give it to them as a wedding present, if you think Amy Lou would like it."

She didn't look at him. "That's a lovely idea. If there's a wedding."

"Yeah?" He ignored the *if* part of her reply.

"Yes."

Oh, hell. He had to get her out of this room. Jake was beside her in six quick strides. He lifted the quilt from her hands and tossed it on the bed, then held out his hand to help her up. Touching her was a mistake, but Jake knew he had to get her out of his bedroom and out of his house before he lost all self-control.

"Come on," he said, his voice gruff. "Let's go into town and get something cold to—" And then he tugged her into his arms and he was kissing a woman who was kissing him back as if she'd been thinking about the same thing he had—hot sex, naked bodies and all the time in the world to enjoy it.

"I don't think we need a storm," she whispered against his lips.

"No, sweetheart," Jake said, tossing her onto the bed. He followed her down and half-sprawled over her while she put her arms around his neck and welcomed him against her. "In fact, it's hotter than hell in here. Why'd you change your mind?"

"I have a good memory," she confessed.

"Yeah," he said. "Me, too."

"It's going to get us in trouble."

"How?"

"I'm not sure." She sighed and reached for his shirt. Unbuttoning each button took an incredibly long time, but Jake figured it was worth it to feel her fingers on his chest. He'd waited a long time for her to touch him again. "But this is going to be a problem."

He sat up, slipped the shirt off his shoulders and tossed it to the floor. "Honey, the only problem we have right now is how to get our clothes off fast enough."

"You think?" she asked, reaching for his belt buckle.

"Yeah." And it turned out to be more of a problem than he figured, Jake realized, what with helping each other and working up a sweat and wanting each other so badly they could barely take time to kick off their shoes. He fell backward on the mattress after getting rid of his boots, and Elizabeth surprised him by climbing over him. Skin like satin moved across his thighs and chest, his penis swelling against her abdomen until she took him in her hand and guided him inside her. She was perfect, tight and hot around him, and he couldn't believe she was on top of him, leaning forward to kiss him as she moved her hips to take every inch of him deep inside.

All in all, Jake figured, this was a pretty good beginning to the evening.

10

"NO MATTER how much you beg, I can't do that a third time."

She opened her eyes and knew she didn't have the energy to do anything but lay in this bed. Making love with Jake had been all-consuming, just as passionate as she remembered. Actually, it was even better than she remembered, if such a thing was possible.

Jake kissed her shoulder and grinned at her. "Honey, if you're looking for a third time before sundown, you're in bed with the wrong Texan." Jake ran his hand down the length of her body, cradling the dip of her waist with his hand. "Of course, we could spend the night here and see what happens."

Elizabeth moved closer to him, despite the high temperature of the room. "Still...we need to get back. Amy will be wondering where we are."

"I doubt it. They're probably out with Bobby's friends, at the Last Chance or maybe even at the Wynette ranch. Bobby's not known for going to bed early. Even your dog's in no hurry to go home."

"Is he okay?"

Jake had brought Pookie and his bed up to the bedroom a while ago, in between making love, because she had worried about the dog being lonely. She'd been surprised Jake understood, but she shouldn't have been. The man's job was taking care of animals.

"He's snoring." Jake gathered Elizabeth into his arms, where she went willingly. "Listen."

Sure enough, the unmistakable sounds of a content Shih Tzu could be heard from the corner. "That's him, all right. He always breathes like that."

"You sleep with him, don't you," Jake commented.

"I'll never tell."

"That's okay," he said. "I don't mind replacing a dog."

She planted a kiss on his chin. "Who says you're replacing him?"

"Sweetheart, there's only room for two of us in this bed, or haven't you noticed?"

Elizabeth snuggled against that hard male body and closed her eyes. "I've noticed," she murmured sleepily. "Wake me up when it's time to go home, okay?"

He could have said, "Sweetheart, we *are* home," but she couldn't be sure. Not when all she wanted to do was stay in this bed and sleep beside her cowboy.

Jake lay awake and worried that this would never happen again, that if he so much as closed his eyes she would disappear the way she had last time. Her gorgeous naked body nestled against his scarred and battered one, her head on his shoulder as she slept.

She was going to stay for the wedding. Maybe. No, she would stay. She loved that niece of hers and she would want to be there when the girl got married. Jake would enjoy seeing that wedding himself, because it meant that at last the caretakers of these kids could start taking care of themselves.

ELIZABETH THOUGHT nothing could surprise her, not after spending the evening in Jake's bed, but the sight of Amy sitting in bed reading a cookbook was something that stopped her in her tracks. She set Pookie, tucked in his bed, on the floor in the hall and went to the door of her niece's room.

"Hi, Aunt B." Her niece, propped against the headboard by a pile of pillows, waved to her. "I've been waiting for you."

"You have?"

"Of course. Where've you been?" She looked at the bedside clock. "It's almost midnight."

Elizabeth couldn't think of one single response and hoped she didn't look too guilty...or too satisfied. Her gaze dropped to the pile of books piled on the bed. "Are you planning tomorrow's meals?"

She sighed. "I'm trying. I have to make a list and then after breakfast Bobby's going to take me to town to get groceries."

"Maybe taking this housekeeping job isn't such a good idea." Elizabeth sat on the edge of the bed and saw *Texas Gourmet: the Best of the West* tipping toward her. "You've never had much experience in the kitchen."

"I never had a reason before now." And held up a book opened to a page displaying plump blueberry pancakes stacked beside scrambled eggs. "Do you think Bobby would like this for breakfast?"

"Anyone would."

"Good." Amy stuck a piece of paper in the book to mark the spot and then tossed it to the floor. "I'll have to get up early, you know."

"I'm sure," Elizabeth agreed, wondering how on earth her very spoiled, very young niece was going to take over the running of a ranch house. It would be a good lesson for her, though, when she realized that there was more to marriage than riding tandem across the prairie into the sunset. "Good night."

"Good night, Aunt B. Thanks for helping me out with the wedding."

Elizabeth hesitated as she got off the bed. "Bobby seems like a very nice young man."

"But?" Amy asked.

"But nothing. If getting married is what you want, then that's what you'll do."

"Really?" Her niece looked a little suspicious, which made Elizabeth smile. "Then you won't oppose the wedding any more?"

"Not if that's what you want. And," Elizabeth added, her voice firm, "I think a bride should plan her own wedding."

"With the help of her mother. Or her aunt," Amy insisted.

"I'll help you." Elizabeth relented. "But you're going to have to make the decisions." And maybe come to the realization that getting married is serious business and not an excuse to throw a great party. "Besides, Amy, what's the rush?"

Amy's cheeks turned pink. "Well, we haven't, um, made love yet."

"Oh." Thank goodness. There was still some sanity involved then, Elizabeth thought, remembering the past hours spent with Jake. At least one of the Comstock women had some self-control.

"And we're both tired of waiting," Amy added. "So the sooner we get married the better."

"I see."

"Do you?" Amy gave her a hopeful look. "I mean, do you really know? Don't you get tired of being by yourself all the time?"

"What do you mean?"

"Don't you want a family, too? I don't mean having kids—I can wait a long time before I do the motherhood thing—but don't you want your own life?"

"I thought I had one."

"But it's just us. I mean, there's just the *two* of us. Everyone else is gone, so here we are."

"In Texas," Elizabeth added, wishing she could run to her own room and crawl into bed this very second. She didn't want to think about having a family or making a life with someone. Being alone felt—well, easier.

"Don't tease. You know what I mean."

Elizabeth backed up a couple of steps. "Of course. but we can talk about it in the morn—"

"Maybe I don't like being alone as much as you do."

Elizabeth tried to ignore the pain that comment caused. "So do you want the cowboy or would marrying anyone be okay?" It was a logical question, considering Amy's propensity for impetuous behavior.

"I like him. A lot."

"But do you love him?"

Amy nodded. "I think so. What about you and Jake?"

"What about it?" Elizabeth was almost out the door, ready to pick up Pookie and make her escape.

"I've seen the way he looks at you," Amy said.

"What do you mean?"

Amy gave her a disgusted look. "Don't tell me you haven't noticed."

"He's a very good-looking man," Elizabeth admitted, praying Amy wouldn't notice that her aunt was blushing.

"And you've kissed him, remember?"

She remembered. How could she forget, when she could still feel his hands on her skin? Elizabeth headed toward the door, but not before her niece asked another question.

"Are you in love with him?"

"Of course not." Which, come to think of it, was not exactly true. She still wasn't sure if what they experienced was lust or infatuation or love, but she really didn't think it was the kind of emotion that led two people to decide to spend the rest of their lives together.

"Here, Auntie." Amy tossed her a cookbook, which Elizabeth caught before it fell to the floor.

"Barbecue: The Way to a Texan's Heart," Elizabeth read aloud. "What's this for?"

"In case you need it."

Elizabeth closed the door on her giggling niece. She scooped up Pookie, bed and all, and didn't realize until she was in her room that she still held the little cookbook in her hand. She set both the book and the dog on her lonely-looking bed before changing into her nightgown. She'd spent several hours making love with and sleeping with a man she barely knew, and yet if anyone asked her if she was in love she would say yes.

Even if she wasn't exactly sure what being in love meant. She knew about grief and responsibilities and dedication. She knew about high school crushes and college coffee dates and even the warm glow of dating a mature man who looked at her as if she was the most beautiful woman he'd ever seen, until he started dating his ex-wife again.

Elizabeth turned up the air-conditioning, spread her flower garden quilt on the bed, rearranged Pookie so he wasn't under the covers—yet—and set the cookbook on the nightstand.

And tried not to dream of the man she'd just made love to.

JAKE WAS LATE getting over to the ranch house. Too many sleepless nights and then making love to Elizabeth last night had caused him to sleep like a dead man until six-thirty. He'd never even heard the alarm at five.

The bunkhouse coffee was gone, so he made a fresh pot and drank two cups while deciding if he'd go on over to the main house and see her before he started work.

Or he could take the day off and have Bobby take care of that shipment of cattle and the meeting with the accountant at eleven. Maybe he'd take the day and paint the inside of his house, make it look like more of a home. It sure hadn't looked like much last night, not that either he or Elizabeth had cared.

Shorty shuffled into the bunkhouse kitchen and helped himself to a cup of coffee. "You're running late today."

"Yeah." Jake finished the last of the coffee in his mug and set it in the sink. "First time in years."

"You goin' anywhere?"

"Why?" Jake asked.

"Figured I'd have to take care of that silly dog of Ms. Comstock's again." Shorty sank down into a battered leather recliner. "I've never seen an animal like that before in my life, 'cept on television."

"Me, either."

"I s'pose they'll be leaving after the wedding?"

"I suppose." Not if Jake had anything to say about it. He thought he'd better find out if Elizabeth was awake or if she'd disappeared. Suddenly he didn't feel so good, as if the bottom of his stomach had fallen right down to his boots.

"The little gal made biscuits," Shorty said. "You'd best get over there before they're all gone."

"Biscuits?"

"Well, sort of, I guess. I can't remember what she called them." Shorty opened yesterday's newspaper and began to read the sports page. "I got that engine oiled up on the tractor, so let me know if you want me to take it over to Dusty at the north ranch."

"Yeah," Jake said, but his thoughts weren't on

tractors or work. He'd made love to Elizabeth last night, and somehow everything in his life had changed.

Maybe that meant he was in love?

Just the thought of it should have scared him, but for some strange reason—maybe because he'd had too much coffee too fast—it only made him walk faster.

He made it to the main house in record time.

"Where's the fire?" Bobby opened the kitchen door. "You almost mowed Gus down."

"That dog of yours shouldn't park himself on the step." He reached over and gave the dog a quick pat of apology before entering the kitchen.

"Stay there, Gus," Bobby told the dog. "I'll bring out some leftovers." He lowered his voice in words meant only for Jake. "Don't eat anything 'cept the scones, no matter what."

"Scones?" Surprised, Jake said the word too loud, which caused Amy to answer.

"There aren't too many left," she said, looking a little harried in Mrs. Martin's oversize apron. The counters were covered with cooking equipment, the smell of burned sausage heavy in the air, and Amy was dusted with flour from head to toe. She didn't seem to notice that the kitchen looked like it had exploded. "But there's still lots of pancakes, if you'd like some."

Jake looked over to the table and saw exactly

whom he needed to see. Immediately, the morning seemed a little brighter, as Elizabeth met his relieved smile with the barest shake of her head. "I'll have a scone, Amy, but I've already had breakfast, thanks," Jake replied.

"Wise man," Elizabeth whispered as he neared the table. Amy had used a flowery tablecloth and stuck a fistful of wildflowers in a vase.

"Sit down," the younger woman called. "I'll bring it over to you."

"You don't have to wait on me," Jake said, while trying to pull out a chair near Elizabeth's without getting the folds of the tablecloth caught on the seat.

"It's my job," Amy said, placing a mug of steaming coffee and a scone in front of him.

"Amy's been up since five," Elizabeth said.

"And you?" Jake wanted to lean across the table and kiss her, just to make sure she was still his. Just to make sure she remembered last night.

"I slept late," she admitted.

"Try the scone things," Bobby urged, pulling up a chair. "They're darned good."

"Okay." Jake picked up the triangle of dough and took a bite. Sure enough, the raisin-dotted biscuit tasted good, but he would have been content with sawdust if Elizabeth had been sitting in the same room. Jake reached for his coffee and hoped he didn't look like a lovesick fool.

A man had his pride, after all.

"I'LL CLEAN UP," Elizabeth volunteered, running water into the sink as Amy stacked the dirty dishes on the counter. The men had gone outside to discuss the work for the day, something about budgets and fences and cattle and horses and all that. Amy decided she would never be much of a horsewoman. Even the thought of riding more that one mile made her thighs ache, and no matter how big the brim of the hat she wore, the sun still gave her a headache.

Amy shook her head. "No. This is my job."

"I can't just sit around and watch you work," Elizabeth said. "Come on, we're in this together. And it was my dog who made Mrs. Martin quit. If you want to do the cooking, fine. But let me help with the dishes, okay?"

"Are you sure?" Amy desperately wanted to prove that she could do it all herself, but she hated washing dishes. Not everything was going to fit in the dishwasher, either, which meant those greasy frying pans with the burned sausages were going to require some scrubbing.

"Yes. Go clean up and start planning your wedding."

"Bobby said he'd take me into town to get things set up, like the food and the place and all that. And I need to get groceries and buy a flour sifter. I couldn't find pure vanilla extract in the cupboard, either. I think Mrs. Martin used the artificial—"

"Amy," her aunt interrupted. "Go."

Still, she hesitated. "Why'd you change your mind last night, Aunt B?"

Elizabeth shrugged. "I thought getting married was another one of your phases, but I can see how happy you are. And how much Bobby loves you."

She *was* happy, especially with a stack of cookbooks to look through. And she had some ideas for tomorrow's breakfast, especially since she wanted to try her hand at yeast dough. Tonight's dessert was going to be the chocolate trifle she saw in the pastry book.

"Did you really like the scones?" Amy asked.

"They were the best I've ever had," her aunt assured her. "Now go get ready. You've got a lot to do if you're getting married in a week."

"I think I'll bake my own wedding cake," Amy declared, heading for the door. "I know I saw a book about it in town and I can make the flowers match the roses in my bouquet."

"You can?" Elizabeth asked with an incredulous expression.

"Of course." Nobody had ever told Amy that baking was this much fun. Or this exciting.

"THAT DIDN'T take long," Dusty said, resting one shoulder against the corral fence.

"I told him if he wanted to get married, I needed more time off to keep the auntie out of the way." Jake would have felt guilty fibbing to Bobby if he

hadn't remembered all the times he'd rescued the
kid at three in the morning when he'd had too much
to drink or lost his keys at the Last Chance or run
out of gas.

Dusty nodded. "Fair enough."

"I told him he could damn well run all the errands in town and do the banking, too. And then, in
his spare time, he could get these horses ready to
sell."

"He'll do all right as boss around here when the
time comes."

"Yeah," Jake agreed. "He's got a lot of his grandfather in him."

"So I hear." Dusty settled his Stetson on his head
and surveyed the horses. "There's a poker game tonight. Are you interested?"

"I doubt it." Jake had other plans for his evening,
and none of them included ranch hands, cards or
the bunkhouse.

Dusty chuckled. "I didn't think you were, but I
thought I'd better ask. Are you and the auntie getting along any better?"

"You might say that."

Dusty turned and raised his dark eyebrows at
Jake. "You're not working today, boss?"

"Not here."

Jake intended to spend the day at his home. And
with his woman. He found Elizabeth up to her el-
bows in soapsuds while singing slightly off-key to a

song on the radio. He took a couple of seconds to admire the curve of her bottom in those shorts before he crossed the room and set his hands on her waist. She jumped and turned, then smiled at him.

"You scared me."

"I didn't know you liked country music," he said, giving her cheek a quick kiss before reaching over to turn the volume down.

"Amy decided she liked to cook while listening to the radio." She turned in his arms and grabbed a dish towel to dry her hands.

"You look very domestic."

"You sound surprised. Didn't you think a math teacher could wash dishes?"

"I guess there's a lot I don't know about you," he said, taking the towel out of her hands. He tossed it onto the counter and then gathered her close. "So, do you want to take the day and get to know each other?"

Elizabeth smiled at him. "And that would mean?"

"Getting out of here, for starters."

"We have a wedding to plan," she reminded him. "I'm not sure Amy and Bobby are going to get it done without our help."

"Amy and Bobby can take care of themselves," he said. "You might want to repeat that to yourself about ten times an hour."

"You're right." She sighed. "I don't know what

happens when I'm with you," she said, tugging his mouth down to hers. "But it's crazy."

"*Good* crazy," he countered, before kissing her for a very long time.

"CAN'T BELIEVE you're here tonight, kid," Shorty drawled, lifting a bottle of beer to his mouth.

Bobby pulled up a chair and sat down. "And I can't believe you're playing poker with a dog on your lap."

"He's okay," Shorty declared, giving the Shih Tzu a pat on the head. "He likes to be with people."

"It looks silly," Bobby insisted. "At least Gus just hangs out beside my chair. On the floor."

"You've no cause to take your bad mood out on the little guy," Shorty declared, but he stopped petting Pookie and picked up his cards. "Sure you're not in, Jake?"

"Not tonight." He'd only stopped by the bunkhouse to give Pookie to Shorty for the evening, since he was taking Elizabeth out to dinner. He was surprised to see Bobby sitting in on the game. "What are you doing here, kid?"

"Amy Lou's practicing with her baking." He looked at his cards and swore. "She's inventing a new dessert."

"She is?"

"Yep. Something with chocolate and whipped cream."

Roy looked up and glared. "Are we playing poker or swappin' recipes?"

Bobby grinned. "Hey, I'm about to win all your money, old man. You in a hurry to lose?"

"Aw, like I believe you," Roy drawled. He flipped a chip into the pile. "I'll take...two cards," he declared, and Dusty dealt them.

"Amy Lou said she'd bring us some of her new dessert later on." Bobby looked around the table. "If you want."

"Sure," Shorty said. "Then she can take this damn dog home with her."

Jake hid a grin. The old man was growing attached to the little dog. And Jake was sure that the attachment went both ways. Elizabeth didn't know it, but her little Shih Tzu liked Texans as much as she and her niece did.

11

SHE FOUND THE LIST when she searched for her clothes on the floor of the bedroom. "Bingo, auction, shopping, quilt show, antiques, tea, canasta." Elizabeth looked over at the cowboy who had just pulled on his jeans. He was entirely too sexy and too appealing for his own good. The urge to tumble him back into bed was almost irresistible, but Elizabeth knew they didn't have much time before they should return to the ranch for dinner. "What's this?"

"The auntie list."

"Really?" She looked at the activities listed. The antique shopping and the quilt show had actually been fun, even though at the time she'd been more than a little nervous in Jake's company. "We didn't do them all."

"Yeah, well, sex wasn't on the list." He sat on the bed and started pulling on his boots, but looked over to smile at her. "At least, not until I saw you standing there in the driveway."

"Neither was painting the living room," she said. "But we did a good job with that, too."

He winced. "Don't remind me. I didn't bring you over here to make you work."

"I like painting." She still had splatters of dried snowflake-white paint on her arms. "And I like your house." She held up the list as she walked over to him. "Were you really going to take me to play bingo?"

"No. I was going to pay Mrs. Martin to do it." He held out his hand and took hers. She went willingly into his arms.

"I think I like this better than bingo," she whispered against his mouth. "And I like you better than Mrs. Martin."

"I like you better than Mrs. Martin, too," Jake said, laughing softly before he kissed her.

Later, while riding back to the Dead Horse in Jake's battered truck, Elizabeth slipped on her sunglasses and watched the flat landscape pass by. Was falling in love really this easy? And if it was, why hadn't she fallen in love before now? Other men had come into her life. Sort of. She turned to look at Jake, all Western male driving his truck and listening to Willie Nelson on the cassette player. They had nothing in common, she reminded herself. They were from two different parts of the country. They had only known each other a few days, unless she counted February. The sudden intimacy last winter, the amazing circumstances that led to seeing him again combined to make her wonder if Fate was trying to tell her something.

She was painting his walls. She'd promised to help pick out scatter rugs at the department store. It was the first time in her life she'd felt safe, as if there was someone to lean on when things went wrong. Jake was the kind of man a woman could depend on, no matter what.

But neither one of them talked about what would happen after the wedding.

"THIS HAS BEEN the best week of my life," Amy declared. She patted dough into tart pans with gentle fingers, lining up the pans in neat rows along the counter. "I never knew I could do anything like this."

Elizabeth took a muffin left over from breakfast and buttered it before sitting down at the kitchen table. "It has?" Amy had burst into tears Tuesday night when she burned her carefully prepared pan of lasagna, prompting Bobby to run into town and bring back pizza. Last night hadn't been much better, with Amy determined to experiment with an apple-topped pork roast. Unfortunately she had forgotten to turn on the oven, so Jake had grilled steaks while Elizabeth put together a salad. The men had eaten pork sandwiches for lunch this afternoon.

"Yes. I never knew dough could be so much fun."
Amy's desserts had been outstanding, so Eliza-

beth easily replied, "You do have a knack for baking. I'm impressed."

Her niece turned and beamed at her. "You are? Really?"

"Of course." The blueberry muffin was the best she'd tasted. Ever. "You know, my grandmother—your father's grandmother—worked in a bakery for years. Maybe you've inherited her talent."

"What was her name?"

"Evelyn," Elizabeth said after thinking a moment. "She's the grandmother who left me the beach house. She must have liked bowls, because the kitchen is full of them."

"Really?"

"Really. I'll pack them up and send them to you when I get back," she promised, and felt a queasiness in the pit of her stomach. She shouldn't have eaten another muffin.

"A bakery," Amy mused. "Where was it?"

"In Providence, I guess." She wiped her hands. "We should go shopping for a wedding dress, Amy. You're running out of time."

"Do you know the name?"

"Of what?"

"The bakery."

"No." Elizabeth got up, went over to the counter and watched, fascinated, as Amy filled the delicate little tarts with apricot filling. "We could drive to Marysville tomorrow morning and shop. It's a good-size town and must have a mall or specialty shops that have long dresses."

"Sure," Amy said, but Elizabeth knew she wasn't really paying attention to a word. This wedding discussion was like trying to push a snowball uphill.

"Is Bobby all set?"

"For what?"

Elizabeth prayed for patience. "For the wedding."

Amy shrugged, her attention focused on something else to cook. "I guess so."

"Have you picked out rings?"

"I told him whatever he got would be fine. Aunt B, do you know how to cook chicken breasts?"

"Yes." So much for the discussion of wedding details. "Is that what you want for dinner?"

"I thought we'd stuff them with spinach and cheese."

"I've never done that, but if you show me the recipe I'll be glad to try. Are the tarts for dessert?"

"Maybe. If they come out okay. I still have a few hours before dinner to make something else."

Elizabeth had no doubt that the tarts would be delicious. At this rate she would gain five pounds before Amy said *I do.* "So, are we all set for tomorrow? I've made a list of the things that still need to be done, so we can talk about that on the drive. Maybe even decide on flowers and let the florist know what you'll need?"

"Sure." Amy reached for another cookbook and opened it to a bookmarked page. "Going to town sounds good. I'd really like to shop for an espresso machine."

Elizabeth didn't know what to say, except to ask when Amy wanted help with the chicken. The bride was certainly taking the art of baking seriously. Too seriously, she thought, sensing trouble. She decided to take Pookie and hunt down Jake. Maybe he would tell her that all ranch wives liked to bake.

She missed him. She hadn't seen him in four hours.

"YOU'RE WORRIED about *what?*" Jake slapped the roan on the rump and sent her running off to join the others in the west pasture. He shoved his hat back and wiped the sweat off his forehead. Elizabeth and the silly dog stood before him. She was as beautiful as ever, and the Pook looked about as dim as he ever did.

"About the wedding," she repeated, those gorgeous green eyes gazing into his. "Amy seems a little too preoccupied with her cooking."

Jake couldn't help laughing. "What are we going to suffer through tonight? Raw bacon and burned fish?"

She smiled. "I'm helping her with chicken. And she's finishing up a few dozen apricot tarts."

His mouth watered just to think of them. "That niece of yours can sure bake."

"She's obsessed."

Elizabeth looked so serious Jake could only smile. He would have taken her into his arms if he wasn't so dirty and if she wasn't holding the hairy dog. Instead he bent down and kissed her. "There's nothing wrong with being obsessed," he said, stripping off his canvas work gloves so he could touch her without getting horse sweat on her.

"No?"

"I feel that way myself sometimes," he murmured, dropping the gloves to the ground.

"Don't try to distract me. I'm really worried," she said, before he kissed her again. She tasted of blueberries and sugar, and Jake's first impulse was to take her home for the rest of the afternoon, but he suspected Elizabeth had other things on her mind besides making love.

"Are there still muffins left?"

She looked confused for a moment, then smiled. "I just ate the last one."

"Damn. Those were sure good this morning." Jake bent over to grab his gloves and took Elizabeth's free hand. He started walking toward the small foreman's house. "What's to be worried about? Amy seems happy enough."

"With baking. I can't get her to do much about the wedding."

"You think she's going to back out?" Just the thought sent a chill down his spine, despite the afternoon heat. As long as Amy was here, Elizabeth would be here. And as long as Elizabeth was here, he had time to figure out what to do.

"I don't know. She'd rather shop for gourmet cooking equipment than a wedding dress. It seems a little...odd, that's all." Elizabeth stopped for a moment to set Pookie on his feet. The little guy looked up at her as if he couldn't believe he had to walk. "Come on," she said, encouraging the little dog to walk with them.

"Bobby hasn't said anything." He slowed his pace to allow for the dog's small steps. The kid had seemed preoccupied these past days, but Jake had chalked that up to pre-wedding jitters. "But I've been keeping him pretty busy with ranch work. There's a lot he has to learn before he takes over."

"You're really going to leave the Dead Horse?"

"Yes," he said, enjoying the feel of her small hand in his. "It's past time for my own home, my own family." He looked over at her, wondering what she would say. It was as close to a proposal as anything he'd ever said, and he waited for her to turn to him and say something.

They must have walked ten feet in silence until she tugged her hand from Jake's and picked up the dog. "Where are we going?"

"I was going to give you a tour of the foreman's

house. It's not much, but there's beer and water in the fridge." He'd messed up big-time. He should have told her he wanted her. He should have told her he was in love with her. He should have asked her to...marry him?

"I can't," she said, backing up a step. "I promised to help Amy with dinner."

"Then I'll see you later," he said, making sure she didn't see his disappointment.

"Sure."

"Beth," he said, before she turned away from him.

"What?"

"You're still so sure this wedding is wrong?"

"I don't want anyone to get hurt."

"Too late," he said.

"Yes. I think it is," Elizabeth answered, a look in her eyes leading him to wonder if they were still talking about Bobby and Amy Lou. He watched her walk away, and he didn't try to stop her.

Maybe she was right. He wanted her to love him. He wanted her to stay. He wanted to build a life and a home. But someone was going to get hurt, and he'd bet a year's pay it was going to be a cowboy.

"WHAT ABOUT this one?" Elizabeth held up a slim ivory gown with narrow straps for Amy's inspection. She had examined racks of gowns this afternoon and had been amazed at the different styles and fabrics.

"It's a little too—I don't know." The bride shrugged her bare shoulders as she stood in the middle of the huge dressing room. "Too simple? It looks like something you would wear, not me."

"How about something like this?" Elizabeth showed her a white gown with embroidered pink roses on the bodice. "You said you wanted flowers."

"It's okay," Amy conceded, taking the hanger and gown. "I'll try it."

The saleswoman poked her head in. "Now remember these gowns are samples. We order the one you choose in the size you need, plus we do alterations."

"The wedding's Monday," Elizabeth told her, and watched the woman blink.

"What size is the bride?"

"Eight," Amy replied, removing the pink-bodiced gown from its satin hanger.

"I'll find our selection of eights for you to see. Would you ladies like something cold to drink?" The saleswoman hovered at the curtained door. "I have refreshments out here in the parlor."

"Thank you," Elizabeth called. "I think we're starting to figure out what styles she likes."

The gray-haired woman chuckled. "It's a long process, honey. Almost as long as finding the groom, so let the bride take her time. And let me know if I can help you in any way."

"Thanks," Elizabeth said, helping Amy into the gown with the pink roses. She zipped up the back and stepped away to look. "You look breathtaking," Elizabeth said. Every dress had looked good on Amy, with her sunny hair and blue eyes. She was shorter than her aunt, and curvier, too. Elizabeth waited for Amy's reaction as she studied herself in the enormous three-way mirror.

"Not bad," the bride declared, lifting her hair up on her head to see what the neckline looked like.

"It's lovely, and you could carry pink roses."

"I wanted yellow," Amy said, smoothing the puffy skirt. "I've been practicing making yellow roses with frosting for the cake."

"I'll see if they have something like it in yellow."

"With thinner straps?" Amy looked as if she was about to cry as she turned away from the mirror and looked at her aunt. "And a skirt that's not so, well, full? I feel like a fool."

"Honey, what's wrong?"

"Oh, Aunt B," she wailed before bursting into tears. "I don't know!"

"Nerves," the saleswoman said from the other side of the curtain. "It happens all the time, honey." The curtain parted a few inches as the woman shoved a handful of tissues into the room. Elizabeth took them and handed them to her niece. Amy wept into the tissues for a few minutes before taking a deep breath and then blowing her nose.

"Let's get you out of that dress," Elizabeth suggested. "I think we'd better take up that offer of a drink."

Amy nodded and wrapped herself in the floral robe provided by Gwen's Gowns. The parlor was a nook around the corner, with wicker chairs and tables. A plate of cookies, bottled tea, a sterling ice bucket, crystal tumblers and a fifth of whiskey sat on a nearby tea cart.

"Sit down, ladies," Gwen said, uncapping the whiskey. She gave Elizabeth a sympathetic smile as she lifted the bottle. "Sometimes the mothers need a little shoring up. Would you like some?"

"Just tea for me." Amy sniffed, but Elizabeth asked for whiskey on ice. Maybe the sight of all those wedding gowns had made her edgy. She wanted to weep along with her niece, but she didn't have the slightest clue why.

"Here you go," Gwen said, serving the drinks before pulling a tapestry-covered stool closer and sitting down. "Sometimes all these choices are too confusing and you have to calm down." She eyed Elizabeth. "Are you the maid of honor?"

"Yes."

"She's my aunt," Amy supplied. "Size ten."

"And you need a dress," Gwen said. "Do you have any special color in mind?"

Elizabeth looked at her niece. "Do I?"

Amy took another sip of her tea and looked as if she was trying very hard not to cry again. "Any color is fine, as long as it's not too practical." She turned to Gwen. "My aunt is very conservative."

"Not really," Elizabeth protested, taking a large swallow of her drink. She had no objection to wearing a drop-dead-gorgeous dress to the wedding.

"I have just the thing." Gwen handed Elizabeth the plate of cookies and walked to the other side of the room. She searched through a rack of pastel dresses until she found what she wanted. "Here," she said, holding out a pale green slip dress. "This subdued shade of jade would be lovely with your coloring. It's a popular color this summer and would go with the yellow the bride prefers." She peered at the tag. "It's a twelve, but this particular company tends to run small."

"Go for it, Aunt B," Amy said.

"Okay," she said, tempted by the simple long sheath. Maybe she could find one of those Victorian-style necklaces to go with it. And pearl sandals with three-inch heels.

Gwen beamed. "I'll put it in the dressing room for you." She scurried off, giving Elizabeth an opportunity to find out exactly why Amy was sniffing into a tissue.

"Amy, for heaven's sake, what's the matter?"

"Nothing." She sniffed again. "Not really. I'm just...I don't know...so confused."

"Do you love him?"

Amy choked back tears and nodded. "I think so. He's really sweet."

"He is," Elizabeth agreed. "But you say that about Pookie, too." She waited for Amy to get control of herself before adding, "Amy, do you still want to get married?"

"It's so different, Aunt B. He's busy all the time and he's talking about having children and I'm more scared of horseback riding than I thought I would be." She stared at her aunt with huge blue eyes before she straightened her shoulders and took a deep breath. "No, that's it. I'm going to buy a dress and I'm going to get married," Amy said, lifting her chin. "I'm determined to grow up and act mature and responsible. Like you."

"I may be mature, but I'm not married," Elizabeth pointed out, reaching for the whiskey bottle. Maybe a tiny bit more would help her cope. She'd tried so hard to forget yesterday. She was so in love with Jake Johnson that when he'd told her he wanted to live in his own home, with his family, she'd held her breath and hoped for...the moon.

They'd never talked of love, never said the words or spoken of the future. Their attraction was based on sex, on chemicals mixing and exploding or something like that. She was mature, but she was crazy.

Amy ignored the comment. "I *do* love him and I'd do *anything* to make him happy."

"Loving him is one thing, Amy. Marrying him is another." She'd be wise to listen to her own advice, she decided, polishing off her drink. She hoped the green dress fit. She wanted to give her own cowboy something to remember.

IT HAD BEEN the strangest week of his life, Jake decided. He almost said it aloud to Pookie, who he was carrying to Shorty for what seemed like the millionth time. The little dog preferred to be with the aging cowboy more than anyone else on the ranch. And this Sunday afternoon Jake was going to take advantage of his day off, so Pookie was off to the bunkhouse again.

"Aw, geez," Shorty wheezed, taking the dog out of Jake's arms. "The little guy's back to disgrace my floor again, is he?"

"He hit a few clods of dirt on the way over. I just carried him the last half of the way," Jake said, trying not to smile. Shorty pretended to grumble about what a nuisance the little runt was, but everyone knew that the old man was going to miss the little guy when Elizabeth left.

If Elizabeth left. Now all Jake had to do was figure out how to get her to stay, but even if he knew what to say and how to say it, he hadn't had many chances to talk to her. He almost suspected she was avoiding him, which made everything so damn hard and confusing.

"I just don't get it," Bobby grumbled, pulling up a chair to the bunkhouse table. "I can't get that woman to pay attention to me."

Jake hesitated before sitting down. He'd promised Elizabeth he'd talk to the kid, but there hadn't been much time to do that in the past few days. And now the wedding was the day after tomorrow. Two of Amy's friends were expected to arrive in town tomorrow, in time for the so-called wedding rehearsal, not that Jake could imagine there was much to rehearse. "You talking about Amy?"

"Yeah." He sighed. "She was crying all over her cooking magazines last night."

Shorty, with Pookie in his arms, went over to the refrigerator and got them all bottles of beer. Dusty entered the room and helped himself to one before sitting down.

"What's going on?" Dusty asked as his beer cap went spinning into the garbage can.

"Wedding jitters," Jake explained, hoping that was all it was.

"You having second thoughts?" Dusty took a long swallow of beer before frowning at Shorty. "You're as bad as the women with that mutt." Pookie was in Shorty's lap at the table, his chin resting on the table's edge as he eyed the men opposite and then yawned.

"He's just fine," Shorty said. "He's right fond of me."

Jake eyed Bobby. "Do you think the bride's having second thoughts?"

"She loves me," the kid declared and glanced at Dusty. "I'm not the one backing out of getting married, but I sure don't know what to do when she's crying."

"Women cry," Jake declared, but his experience was limited to memories of his mother. "That's just what they do."

"Yeah," Dusty said. "Jake's right."

"The women got dresses, right?"

Bobby nodded. "Yeah. And a bunch of other stuff, too. Amy Lou's been making me drink coffee from little cups. She bought some kind of special coffee machine." He sighed and looked as if he was being tortured. "I thought being married was going to be fun."

"You did?" Dusty exchanged glances with Jake, who clapped the young man on the shoulder.

"I'm taking the aunt to an auction this afternoon," Jake said. "So you'll have time to talk to your bride and get this straightened out."

"You think I should?"

"You're running out of time," Jake told him. "And you'd better be damn sure that you're doing the right thing before you say I do on Tuesday." He finished his beer, scraped back his chair and caught

Shorty's eye. "We might be late, so hang onto the dog until I get back."

"Thanks, Jake," Bobby said. "For taking care of the aunt and everything."

"No problem." He pretended not to see the grin Dusty shot his way as he left the building. He was going to entertain the auntie, all right. And then he was going to ask her to marry him.

12

"YOU WANT to go for a ride?"

"On a horse?"

"Sure," Bobby said, looking a little confused. "Or we could take the truck and just ride around town for a while. We could go get a steak or something."

"That's okay," Amy said, wishing she could be alone for a while longer. Her fiancé wasn't about to give up. Instead he lingered in the kitchen and looked nervous. "I don't need to go anywhere."

"You want to talk about what's goin' on?"

Amy shook her head and tossed the new issue of *Bon Appetit* into the wastebasket. "I'm fine. Honest."

Bobby walked across the kitchen and, ignoring the tempting platter of cream puffs next to the stove, plucked the magazine out of the garbage. Amy watched as he found the page in the middle section, the one she'd marked by turning down the corner. "What's this?"

Amy didn't answer. She didn't want to hurt the nicest man she'd ever been in love with by telling him that she would rather learn how to make profiteroles or perfect *crêpes soufflés au citron* than ride off into the sunset with an adorable cowboy.

"Paris?" He tried to smile, and attempted a joke. "I guess that doesn't mean Paris, Texas."

"It's not important," Amy said. "Really."

"You got any of that coffee left?"

Relieved to have the subject changed, Amy pushed Bobby toward the table. "Sure. Sit down. I'll bring you a cream puff, too. Do you want one with whipped cream or vanilla pudding?"

"Doesn't matter," he said, setting the open magazine on the table in front of him. "I'll bet either one will be real good."

"I hope so," Amy said, setting coffee and dessert in front of him. She couldn't help feeling proud of herself for succeeding on her first attempt. The cream puffs looked almost exactly like the ones in the *Provincial France* cookbook.

"Jake took your aunt to an auction on the other side of town," he said, picking up his fork. "I guess she's helping him get some furniture for his house."

"She's good at stuff like that." Amy hesitated before joining Bobby at the table. She tried not to look at the magazine, its page opened to the article on the famed Parisian baking school. Just the pictures made her uncomfortable.

"Like you're good at baking," he said, pulling the magazine closer and taking a big forkful of cream puff.

"I finished the wedding cake," she announced, deliberately avoiding looking at the magazine. Instead she watched Bobby enjoy the dessert she'd created. "It's in sections, in the freezer. Of course I'll defrost it before frosting it tomorrow night."

"This summer session at the baking school starts in three days," he said.

"I decided on yellow frosting," she continued, fighting back tears. "Did I tell you I bought the dress to match? It's a Paloma Blanca design with embroidered gold—"

"Geez, Amy Lou," Bobby sputtered. "Are you gonna start crying again or are you gonna tell me what's going on? You haven't said much to me this week except to ask me if I wanted seconds on something. And your eyes get all red and you're always in the kitchen, which has its advantages because your muffins are the best in the county, but you're avoiding me and we're supposed to be getting married the day after tomorrow."

Amy took a deep breath and decided that a little bit of truth was better than all of it. How could she tell him that she dreamed more about a degree in cuisine from a Paris cooking school than producing little Calhoun cowboys and cowgirls? How could she do something horrible like hurt this man she really thought she was in love with? She was determined this time to stick with her plans and not be impulsive. "It's just that...I've never been good at anything until now. Oh, I'd like to think I was good at acting and screaming at jellyfish and writing poems and all that, but I wasn't really." She tried to smile, but her eyes burned with unshed tears. "It's really not fair."

He stood up and went over to her, pulling her into his embrace. "What isn't, honey?"

"That Le Cordon Bleu isn't in Paris, Texas." She wept a little against his checked shirt before pulling away to dig a tissue out of her shorts pocket.

"I hate it when women cry," Bobby grumbled, releasing her and jamming his hands in his pockets. "We *are* getting married, aren't we?"

"Sure." She sniffed.

"Honey, you don't sound real enthusiastic." He smiled at her. "I don't want you to do anything you're not one hundred percent sure about."

"Are you sure?" She held her breath and waited for the answer.

"I'm sure I want you to be happy," Bobby said, and took her into his arms. "And I'm going to make sure you are."

"DO YOU WANT IT or not?" Elizabeth whispered.

"What do you think?"

"It'll fit," she assured him, keeping her attention focused on the auctioneer. "And it's solid." She held up her numbered card and raised the bid to sixty-five dollars. Someone in back went to seventy-five, and Elizabeth hesitated. It was Jake's money and Jake's house, and if the man didn't realize a bargain when he saw one, so be it.

"Do it," he said, so she raised the bid again.

"How high do you want to go?"

"You decide."

She bought the massive pine farm table for one hundred and fifteen dollars, which she considered a bargain. She wasn't so sure that Jake did, but she knew once he saw it in his freshly painted dining room he'd be pleased. Fifteen minutes later she bid on and won six chairs to go with the table, plus a bench that would look great painted and sitting on the porch.

"Okay," she said, examining the list of notes she'd made before the auction began. They'd arrived at the auction barn with enough time to examine just about everything before the auctioneer held up the first item. "Is there anything else you need?" She turned toward him and smiled when his brows lifted in amusement.

"I can think of something," he drawled.

Why did her insides melt when he looked at her like that? Elizabeth fanned herself with her bidding card. "I meant here, at the auction."

"I can't think of anything."

She looked at the list. "I wish we'd gotten those rocking chairs for the porch."

"A rancher doesn't have much time for sitting in rocking chairs."

"You liked those rugs," she said, wondering if they would go high. "I wish I knew more about rugs and what's good and what's not."

"I can get them new in town."

"I suppose." She drew a line through "192—blue rugs." "What about the old tool chest you were looking at?"

For a second Jake seemed tempted, then shook his head. "I can get tools at Sears. Let's go home." He hesitated. "Unless there's something you want to stay and bid on."

"No." She liked auctions but she liked going home with Jake a lot better. She'd managed to bury herself in wedding plans since the last time she and Jake talked, but the simple truth was she missed him. Missed being with him. Missed talking to him. Missed making love to him.

What on earth was she going to do with herself for the rest of the summer? She'd fallen in love with the man. She'd been in love with him since last winter, that love-at-first-sight feeling she'd so often scoffed at. And now here she was, waiting by the new table in the back of the barn for Jake to pay for his furniture so they could take it to his house. Take it *home*, he'd said.

But it wasn't her home, and she didn't know how to turn a brief love affair into something permanent.

Not when they were so different. Not when this could all be chalked up to love, to infatuation, even—and most embarrassing—to loneliness.

At least that's what she told herself as she stood there watching the tall rancher pick up his receipt from the woman at the desk. And she kept telling herself so when Jake gave her the keys to the truck and asked her to bring it to the door so he and some of the other men could load the table into the back.

Elizabeth was thrilled with herself, and decided backing up a truck was a heck of a lot easier than steering a horse. She helped load the chairs, too, despite the men's assurances that they could do it.

"Looks like your wife's pretty happy with her new table," one of the older men said to Jake.

"Sure is," was Jake's reply, though Elizabeth pretended she didn't hear the comment. "Let's hope she likes it when we get it home," he told the men, then thanked them for the help.

"It fits," she announced an hour later. Jake had wanted to stop at the ranch and get one of the men to help unload the truck, but Elizabeth thought they could do it together.

"I told you so." She stood with her hands on her hips and admired the room. "It's perfect."

"Yes." Jake lifted her by the waist and sat her on the table. "Now kiss me, Aunt B. It's been too damn long."

What could she do? The man was right.

"OH, MY GOD! Aunt B? What are you doing?"

Jake opened his eyes to see Bobby and Amy Lou standing in his bedroom doorway. Elizabeth let out a little shriek and pulled the covers over her bare shoulder.

"What the hell—" Jake began, but Bobby interrupted.

"Oh, jeez, Jake, I'm sorry. We were looking for you but I never thought—"

"I thought you were *painting*," Amy said. "And you're doing—this."

"Amy, please—"

The young woman continued to stare at them. "We've been looking for you everywhere. This was *important*."

And this wasn't? Jake didn't dare look at Elizabeth. She was either stunned speechless or in a state of shock. He knew this was her worst nightmare come true. "You could've knocked," he pointed out.

"We did," Bobby said, trying to tug Amy into the hallway, but the young woman wasn't having any of it. "I guess you didn't hear with, uh, the fan going and all."

So buying a big fan hadn't been such a good idea, after all, Jake thought. "Maybe we should meet you two back at the ranch."

"Aunt B," Amy said, giving her fiancé a quick kick in the shins so he'd stop dragging her. "I *really* need to talk to you."

"Not now," Elizabeth said, sounding as if she was clenching her teeth. Jake glanced at her and saw a woman with flushed cheeks and tousled hair, a woman who looked nothing like a conservative New England math teacher. She was beautiful, she was his, and she wasn't going anywhere. He turned to the youngsters.

"You heard the lady," he said, giving Bobby his sternest look. "Go back to the ranch and we'll see you there in a while."

"You don't understand," Amy wailed. "I need to tell—"

"Go," he repeated, and this time Bobby successfully removed Amy from the doorway. The young man turned to Jake and gave him a pleading look.

"Could you hurry?" Bobby asked. "We're sort of in a rush."

"We'll hurry," Elizabeth promised.

"No, we won't," Jake said, and then they were gone as silently as they had come in, except this time Jake heard the front door open and shut. "I guess buying that fan was a bad idea."

"Along with not locking the doors."

"I was distracted." Jake had been too busy wondering if he should make love to Elizabeth on the tabletop or in the bed. They'd managed to do both, and lucky for them they were half-asleep when they discovered they had guests. If Bobby and Amy had appeared fifteen minutes earlier, it would have been really embarrassing.

"I am so embarrassed. I'm supposed to be setting a good example, not sleeping with cowboys." Elizabeth tossed back the sheet and started to leave, but Jake turned and caught her arm.

"Cowboys?" he echoed. "Plural?"

"Quit teasing," she told him. "We've got to get out of here."

"Elizabeth, you're a grown woman. Surely you're allowed to have a sex life."

"In front of my virgin niece? I don't think so." She rose up enough to give him a quick kiss and then scooted out of the bed. "Come on. I think something's really wrong."

"If it was an emergency they would have waited downstairs," he insisted, but Elizabeth was halfway across the room picking up her underwear. Jake leaned against the pillow and closed his eyes for one brief moment. This time Elizabeth wasn't tiptoeing from his bed while he was asleep, but he had the sinking feeling that she was leaving him just the same.

MARTY SHRUGGED. "I dunno, Ms. Comstock. They lit out of here really fast."

Elizabeth hopped down from the truck and gave Gus an absent pat on the head as he greeted her. It had taken too long to return to the ranch and they'd missed Amy and Bobby. The trip seemed longer because of the silence that had stretched between Elizabeth and Jake the entire way. There didn't seem to be anything to say until they talked to Bobby and Amy. "How long ago?"

"Ten, fifteen minutes," one of the twins said, holding onto her horse's reins. "We were just coming back from a ride and we said hi, what's up, and Amy Lou said something about leaving."

"Leaving? To go to town?" Elizabeth asked.

The twin on the left brightened. "Maybe she was going home, you know, to Rhode Island."

The other twin shook her head. "I bet they were eloping."

Marty shook his head. "Nope. Bobby didn't look real happy."

"Eloping?" Elizabeth echoed. "Why would they do that when they're supposed to get married in two days?" She turned to Jake. "Do you know anything about this?"

"Only the kid said Amy had been crying a lot." Jake frowned. "Do you think she's called the wedding off?"

Elizabeth didn't know what to say. "I hope not," she told him, but he looked skeptical. "But nothing Amy did would surprise me."

Jake swore under his breath and looked down the drive as if he expected to find all the answers in the empty road. "Well, I can't say you didn't warn me."

"I'm sorry."

"Yeah. Me, too." Then, realizing that the twins and Marty were staring at them, he took Elizabeth's arm and drew her aside. "I guess I should have believed you when you said this would never work. You said this was no life for your niece."

Her heart landed in her abdomen as she saw the bitterness in his expression. "I didn't—"

"Cooking and cleaning and living far from town and having babies, I think that's how you described it," he said, his voice rough. "I guess Amy Lou finally figured out that you were right all along."

"I didn't want to be right." Elizabeth wanted to be wrong about cowboys and Eastern women, wanted to believe that love conquers all. She put her hand on Jake's arm.

"Everyone's different," she said, wishing with all her heart he would ask her to stay with him. She'd love the babies and the cooking, tolerate the cleaning and maybe even substitute teach at the high school once in a while if she discovered she missed working. She wanted to spend her days and her nights on that ranch, with that rancher, under those quilts.

He wouldn't even look at her, so she dropped her hand and turned toward the house. He was angry the wedding was canceled, she realized. Disappointed that his plans for his ranch would have to wait. And anxious to be rid of her now that the wedding was off. Her job as chaperone was finished and so was their brief affair.

She hurried to the ranch house, hoping to find a written explanation on the kitchen table. Since there was no note in the kitchen, Elizabeth headed upstairs and prayed that Amy hadn't done anything foolish. Surely this latest drama had something to do with the wedding—something simple, such as the wrong flowers had been ordered or the Steak Barn had mixed up their menu.

The door to Amy's room stood open, and the note was on the bed.

"Aunt B," it read. "Don't be mad. I'll call you soon." It was signed with a familiar rounded A and a little heart. The closet door was open, Amy's few clothes gone with the exception of the beautiful wedding dress, still encased in plastic. The suitcase was no longer on the floor under the window.

Elizabeth blinked back the sting of tears. Would a bride elope without her new dress? No way.

Amy was gone. Bobby would be heartbroken. Jake was furious. She had wanted to believe that love at first sight could blossom into something lasting, that strangers could find each other again and live happily ever after. She had even started to think she might make a good ranch wife.

The romance was over. It was time to get out of Texas, after all.

"HE WUZ takin' her to the airport," Shorty said, carrying Pookie to a patch of grass near the door as Jake approached the bunkhouse. Shorty set the little dog down and watched him sniff around. "That's all he said, Jake."

"I don't suppose he was going with her?"

Dusty stuck his head out the door. "You're looking for Bobby? He took off a little while ago."

"Didn't have nothing with him," Shorty said, picking up Pookie after he'd lifted his leg and returned to the old man's feet. "'Cept the little gal's suitcase. They took the Caddy and took off, dust flyin' everywhere."

"Yeah," Dusty added. "He told me to tell you he'd be back later, but they were going to miss the plane if they didn't leave right away."

"Damn it all to hell." Jake wanted to break something. He wanted to put his fist through the window. And then he wanted to get very, very drunk.

"Here." Shorty blinked back tears and put Pookie in Jake's arms. "I expect the auntie will be wanting to take him with her when she leaves, huh?"

"I guess," Jake replied. So the wedding was off. Bobby must be real broken up, Elizabeth was getting exactly what she wanted all along and he was left holding the dog.

IT TOOK HER nine minutes to call the airline, shower and pack. She saved time by crying in the shower, lost time by trying to put makeup on while weeping. The packing was a mess. She managed to stuff the green gown into an already bulging suitcase, because she couldn't bear to leave it behind as Amy had left hers. The quilt went into a shopping bag she would carry on the plane along with the dog crate.

Jake was waiting for her in the kitchen when she came downstairs. Pookie, his topknot askew, sat in his little bed by the back door and gazed at her with his typical sweet, vacant expression.

Jake glanced at her suitcase, his jaw clenched. His hat was low on his forehead, casting a shadow over his eyes that made it hard to read his expression. "That was fast."

"There was a note saying she was sorry, but she left her wedding dress," she said, smoothing her damp palms on her skirt, the same skirt she'd worn when she'd arrived at the Dead Horse. "I don't think they've eloped. I think Amy's gone home."

Jake crossed his arms in front of his chest, almost as if he was barring the door. "I know. Shorty said Bobby's taken her to the airport."

"Oh." Of course the other ranch hands would know what was going on. "I called the airline. The next flight to Providence leaves in two hours and forty-three minutes."

She waited for him to say something, anything, but he remained silent. "It's a two-hour drive," she said, hoping he wouldn't notice the way her voice quavered. "I guess we'd better get on our way." He stepped forward and took her suitcase while she gathered Pookie, his travel cage and his bed. Jake paused halfway out the door.

Please, she wanted to say. *Please ask me to stay. Tell me you love me. Tell me anything.*

"I figured you'd want to leave," Jake said. "Dusty's going to drive you," he said, not looking at her. He set her suitcase in the back of one of the ranch pickup trucks while Dusty helped her and Pookie get settled in the front seat. Jake came around to the passenger side and leaned in. She thought he was going to kiss her, but she couldn't bear to say goodbye that way. If he kissed her goodbye she would burst into tears and embarrass both of them.

If he kissed her goodbye she would never leave.

"Jake?"

He waited for her to get her seat belt on and settle Pookie in his bed at her feet before he shut the door.

"He'll come around," Dusty assured her as he backed up the truck and turned around. He shifted gears, and the truck bounced along the drive away from the ranch. "I've got a bet going that says there's going to be a wedding."

"How much?"

"A hundred bucks," the cowboy replied.

"Well," Elizabeth said, her voice shaky as she

watched the fence posts past by. "I hope you're feeling luckier than I am."

She was on time for the plane to Providence, though Dusty had to stop for gas and didn't drive over the speed limit. Elizabeth assumed he was trying to protect his hundred dollars and was hoping for a miracle. The only miracle was her being able to convince the cowboy to drop her off at the proper terminal and leave her bags to the airport valet to carry, while Pookie relieved himself against a cement post. Then she and Pookie, tucked in his crate, navigated the ticket counter, the security check and journey to the correct gate.

"She's not here." The voice drawled from behind her. Bobby grinned when she turned around. "She figured you'd be here. I just put her on a plane to Paris."

"Paris?" Elizabeth noticed the young cowboy didn't look devastated. In fact, she thought, he looked pleased with himself. "Why?" she asked.

"To go to some fancy baking school," he replied, reaching out to take Pookie's crate from her. "Class starts in two days. You want to sit down? You look kinda flushed." He led her to a row of empty seats by the window overlooking her airplane.

"But her passport—"

"She brought it with her to Texas, on account of not knowing what we were gonna do for a honeymoon."

"Oh, Bobby, I'm sorry. Are you very disappointed?"

"Maybe a little," he said, resting the crate on his lap. "Is it okay if I take him out or will we get in trouble?"

"I don't think anyone will mind." She watched as he unhooked the door and the dog peeked out, stretching his paws in front of him. "Bobby, what's going on?"

"I couldn't stand to see her so sad, Ms. Comstock. And she wanted to give up baking in order to get married and not hurt me, but I just wouldn't allow it. We're gonna keep in touch and see what happens next year, after she's got her degree in pastry. She asked me to hang on to the dress, just in case."

"That's very...civilized," Elizabeth told him, watching as he scratched Pookie's ears and surveyed the travelers sauntering past. "I hope it works out."

"Well, thanks. And I hope everything works out for you, too. Shorty sure is fond of this dog." He handed Pookie to her and stood up, tipping his hat to someone behind her.

"I remembered that I owe you a quilt," someone said, and when she turned, of course there was Jake. He stood there holding one of his mother's quilts, the ivory one with tiny pieces of pastel fabrics stitched together in intersecting circles.

Elizabeth was afraid to move. He looked so handsome and so upset, but his face relaxed when Bobby grinned at him and clapped him on the shoulder.

"I think I'll go get a great big ol' cup of coffee," the young man said, leaving them alone.

"What are you doing?"

"I drove ninety miles an hour to get here before you left." He tossed the quilt over the seat next to her. "It's the wedding ring pattern. I thought it was appropriate, considering."

"Considering?"

"The bet we made. In that antique shop. You said there wouldn't be a wedding and you won." He shoved the quilt aside and sat down as if he didn't have a care in the world.

"I didn't want to win," she whispered, as his arm stretched out behind her shoulders. If she moved over a few inches she could rest her head on his shoulder. Pookie snuggled deeper into her arms and began to snore.

"You haven't. Yet. If there *is* a wedding you owe me a date at the drive-in."

"They're not getting married. Not yet."

"The bet was for a wedding," he countered. "We didn't specify whose. Honey, I spent ten minutes without you and thought I was going to die of a broken heart. I don't care how different we are or that we've only known each other a little while or anything else. I'm not going to let you leave here without knowing that I'm in love with you and that's not going to change, no matter what. So either you marry me and stay here or you marry me and we go East." He pointed to a battered leather bag. "I packed, just in case. And I have a ticket, too. So what do you say?"

"I say..." she said, turning to face him so that their lips were only inches apart. "I want the quilt." Her lips brushed his. "And the wedding." Another brush of lips. "And the ranch." He started kissing her back, but she had to add, "And the cowboy." She would have kissed him for hours, but Pookie barked his discomfort at being squished between two lovers. "So," she said, when they had separated enough to satisfy the little dog. "What do you say?"

A satisfied Texan scooped up the quilt, the woman, the bags and the dog. "I think, lady, it's going to be one hell of a night."

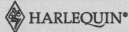

You're not going to believe this offer!

In October and November 2000, buy any two Harlequin or Silhouette books and save $10.00 off future purchases, or buy any three and save $20.00 off future purchases!

Just fill out this form and attach 2 proofs of purchase (cash register receipts) from October and November 2000 books and Harlequin will send you a coupon booklet worth a total savings of $10.00 off future purchases of Harlequin and Silhouette books in 2001. Send us 3 proofs of purchase and we will send you a coupon booklet worth a total savings of $20.00 off future purchases.

Saving money has never been this easy.

I accept your offer! Please send me a coupon booklet:

Name: _____

Address: _____ City: _____

State/Prov.: _____ Zip/Postal Code: _____

Optional Survey!

In a typical month, how many Harlequin or Silhouette books would you buy <u>new</u> at retail stores?

☐ Less than 1   ☐ 1   ☐ 2   ☐ 3 to 4   ☐ 5+

Which of the following statements best describes how you <u>buy</u> Harlequin or Silhouette books? Choose one answer only that <u>best</u> describes you.

    ☐ I am a regular buyer and reader
    ☐ I am a regular reader but buy only occasionally
    ☐ I only buy and read for specific times of the year, e.g. vacations
    ☐ I subscribe through Reader Service but also buy at retail stores
    ☐ I mainly borrow and buy only occasionally
    ☐ I am an occasional buyer and reader

Which of the following statements best describes how you <u>choose</u> the Harlequin and Silhouette series books you buy <u>new</u> at retail stores? By "series," we mean books within a particular line, such as *Harlequin PRESENTS* or *Silhouette SPECIAL EDITION.* Choose one answer only that <u>best</u> describes you.

    ☐ I only buy books from my favorite series
    ☐ I generally buy books from my favorite series but also buy
       books from other series on occasion
    ☐ I buy some books from my favorite series but also buy from
       many other series regularly
    ☐ I buy all types of books depending on my mood and what
       I find interesting and have no favorite series

Please send this form, along with your cash register receipts as proofs of purchase, to:
In the U.S.: Harlequin Books, P.O. Box 9057, Buffalo, NY 14269
In Canada: Harlequin Books, P.O. Box 622, Fort Erie, Ontario L2A 5X3
(Allow 4-6 weeks for delivery) Offer expires December 31, 2000.   PHQ4002

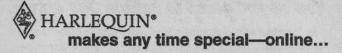

has a brand-new look!

**Still offering favorite authors such as
Muriel Jensen, Judy Christenberry,
Tina Leonard and Cathy Gillen Thacker.**

**Look for
Harlequin AMERICAN *Romance*
at your favorite retail outlet in November 2000.**

HARNEW00